Love Lasts Longest

Longest

Alternate Short Tales of
Pride and Prejudice

Rose Fairbanks

Love Lasts Longest

Published by Rose Fairbanks

©2015 Rose Fairbanks

Early drafts of this work were posted online.

Several passages in this novel are paraphrased from the works of Jane Austen.

This is a work of fiction. Any resemblance to characters, whether living or dead, is not the intention of this author.

Dedication

To Aunt J who first told me that books were a magical escape. To Aunt L who gave her favorite childhood books to my hungry eyes. To my husband who reads every book I write and to my children who love to read as much as I do.

Under the Apple Tree

I grew up in the mountains of Virginia. Few things capture the comfort of autumn like a good apple does.

October 1811

Longbourn, Hertfordshire

"Ruined! What do you mean ruined?"

Elizabeth rounded a corner and heard her mother shrieking.

"We will be turned out before Mr. Bennet is cold in his grave. There is no hope! Why bother with it at all then?"

Usually given to ignore her mother's cries, Elizabeth felt the current complaints a bit more genuine. "Mama, what has happened?"

"Cook says the pastry for dessert I planned is ruined, and Mr. Bingley and the rest of the Netherfield party is to arrive any moment. There is no time to bake anything else. Mr. Bingley will see that I cannot host a proper meal and turn his attentions elsewhere. Why, Lady Lucas and Mrs. Long would just love that!"

"Mama, I hardly think Mr. Bingley would decide upon which lady to marry given one meal at her family's house."

"Oh! What do you know of these things? A man always looks to the mother to see how the daughter will fare. If I cannot keep a proper table, then he will believe Jane ignorant as well."

Elizabeth's eyes widened in fear. Not that she worried Mr. Bingley would reject Jane on the lack of dessert, but she sincerely prayed gentlemen would not accept or reject her and her sisters due to the behaviour of her mother.

Mrs. Bennet sobbed into her handkerchief. Desperate to cheer her, Elizabeth thought quickly.

Patting her mother's arm, Elizabeth soothed her. "Hush, Mama. I will go and gather some apples before the party arrives. Surely Cook can make something with them. It will be a charming country finish to your other elegant courses. He will see that Jane would be the perfect mistress to either his country or London house."

"No! You will return covered in dirt and not be fit to be seen. I shall send a servant."

"Can you spare them? Are they not all busy below stairs and Susie dressing Jane?"

"Very well, but do not tarry, and be careful of the mud!"

Elizabeth gathered up her outdoor clothes and smiled to herself. The near catastrophe in the kitchens served to excuse her from the house as her mother fretted over Mr. Bingley's arrival. He would bring Mr. Darcy with him, and although Elizabeth had only known him about a fortnight and seen him in company three times since their first meeting, she was beginning to believe he was the most arrogant man who ever lived. He would not smile or laugh, he would barely speak, and when he did, it was condescending. He clearly had no wish to be amongst them, believing himself so superior. Why did he come at all? Poor Mr. Bingley to have such a sour friend.

Elizabeth giggled to herself. Near the house, they only had one apple tree, and the fruit was sour eaten raw but delicious when cooked. She would like to offer one to

Mr. Darcy; perhaps that would finally elicit some kind of reaction from him. If nothing else, she could laugh at him.

She approached the tree but was dismayed to find that many apples were already plucked and no fresh ones on the ground. Looking up she shrugged her shoulders. There was really only one option.

*****

Darcy sat in Longbourn's parlour, annoyed. Bingley had been overeager to arrive for the dinner and came above an hour early. Mrs. Bennet was shriller in her own home, the younger girls sillier at each encounter, and he would wager that Mr. Bennet was content to laugh at them all. Bingley and the eldest Miss Bennet were sitting together and talking.

He rolled his eyes. His friend was besotted again, but he had no fear of it lasting more than the usual few weeks. What could possibly attract his attention longer? That the Bennets could not improve Bingley's situation in life was rather clear. She was a gentleman's daughter, but he already knew of their poor connections. Miss Bingley was quick to learn the details on all their neighbours. As for her charms...well, she was classically beautiful but smiled too much, seemed to hold little opinion on any matter, had no wit, and did not appear to play an instrument or sing. Mrs. Bennet was the sort to make the most out of what her daughters had to attract a suitor, and it was rather clear she believed her eldest daughter's greatest asset was her beauty. He shook his head at the notion of marrying over such a transient thing. What a fool a man would be to do so! Yet others before him had done as much.

Caroline and Louisa would usually be excruciatingly cloying for his attention but instead sat silently, taking everything in to criticise later. There was a decided lack of sense in the room. Where was Miss Elizabeth?

He was annoyed that his thoughts drifted to her. She attracted him more than he liked. Only a few days ago he determined her scarcely pretty, and now it seemed every time he even glanced at her she grew in beauty. Presently he could not understand it at all, but he was rather certain only a fortnight ago he believed her figure flawed and her manners too unpolished. Now he admitted to anticipating their meetings. He shook his head and tried to hide the mortification he felt at his thoughts. Did he not just think men fools for marrying based only on attraction? Although surely his thoughts did not tend toward marriage, he admired her, that was all. She was lovely, intelligent, and witty. Knowing her other family, he could hazard a guess how strong her character was to better herself so much. Mrs. Bennet offered a tour of the home, and Darcy used the moment of distraction to slip out of doors.

Walking around the small park, he espied a very fine old tree, picked of most of its apples, which provided nice shade. Glancing at his watch, he estimated that he could enjoy nearly half an hour of peace. So he sat and pulled out a book of sonnets he carried with him when he had moments of leisure. He hated standing in idleness or being left to converse with strangers.

He had just settled himself when he heard a bit of a shriek and, looking up, saw a white blur tumbling down. Before he could react, a heavy basket dropped on his head.

The next thing Darcy saw was the worried expression in Elizabeth Bennet's beautiful eyes. He was no longer sitting, but instead sprawled out below the tree. The hit to the head must have caused him to briefly lose consciousness.

"Mr. Darcy! Can you hear me now?" She was speaking very loudly.

"My hearing is quite fine, Miss Bennet."

"Then you are well? After the basket fell, you seemed unconscious for a moment. No one ever told you not to sit under an apple tree?"

He slowly shook his head, groaning a little while feeling bits of apple on him. Some bitter juice invaded his mouth, and he scowled. He began to pick himself clean, and Elizabeth stifled a laugh. He looked up at her expectantly.

"Forgive me, sir." She again stifled a laugh.

"I understand you find this amusing?"

"It is only that this is the first time I have seen you express much of anything since the Assembly."

"Since the Assembly?"

"I have said too much. How is your head?"

"I feel a bit like a basket of apples fell on it." She laughed outright at that, and Darcy was surprised to feel his pulse race. Not only was her beauty unparalleled at such a moment, but he knew to make this woman laugh was a privilege denied to most.

"Can you get up?" she asked, and he had to clear the fog of his thoughts.

"I believe so." He glanced up at the tree as he began to stand, hiding an expression of pain.

"Since you have had the pleasure of laughing at me, Miss Bennet, I rather hope you could answer what you and your basket were doing up there."

Elizabeth blushed prettily but laughed as well. "I was collecting apples for our dessert as some catastrophe befell the pastry Mama had ordered. She is vexed beyond compare over it."

"So you were the dutiful daughter to pick apples? Now, were you simply the first to be dressed, or are you the best tree climber?"

"You tease very well, sir! In truth, I am the dutiful *sister*. Mama wishes to impress Mr. Bingley, and I wish to help for Jane's sake."

He was a bit surprised that Mrs. Bennet did not wish to impress him, but Elizabeth was likely wise enough to know not to mention it to him. Still, he mumbled, "I am certain there are five thousand reasons to impress Bingley."

Her eyes flashed. "Jane thinks Mr. Bingley is the most amiable gentleman she has ever met, and I assure you, it is through understanding his character that she likes him more with each meeting. You will think us simpletons, but I speak for myself and all my sisters when I say we wish to marry for companionship and affection. While I hope we would never be imprudent with money, our dearest wish is for friendship in marriage."

Feeling thoroughly chastised, he could only nod his head. Taking out his watch, he acknowledged the tour was likely over and dinner about to begin. Seeing the basket was battered, he found his hat, then gathered the intact apples.

"We should return." He held out his hand to help Elizabeth stand and could not miss her grimace as she put weight on her feet. "Forgive me, I did not ask if you were injured."

"I did not know that I was. It is only a twisted ankle, I am sure. Not my first."

"Nor your last?"

"Contrary to what you believe of me, Mr. Darcy, I am seldom in the practice of climbing trees," she said testily, but he would not have it.

"In the last…three years?"

Despite her previous annoyance, she let out a light laugh. "You have found me out. Mama put me out at fifteen, but I indulged myself in childish pursuits on occasion until I felt I really must grow up."

He laughed. "I am pleased to hear it. I have a sister who is just fifteen. I can no longer deny she is nearly grown, but I enjoy thinking of her as having some youthful innocence still." He pushed away thoughts of his father's godson, George Wickham, nearly eloping with her. "Can you walk if you lean on my arm?"

She placed her gloved hand on his arm, and he would have been embarrassed at the feelings he felt if he did not see her cheeks turn pink as well.

"We shall go slowly."

She nodded, but he could see her struggle with each step. Putting aside his own discomfort, he chose to talk.

*****

Elizabeth was surprised to find Mr. Darcy so friendly and obliging, even teasing.

"I think I would wish my sister as fearless as you. She was always a very cautious child. Neither of us were given to levity," he said.

"And now?"

"She has recently seemed to exercise her opinion in a more…adult way."

"Your poor mother. It is a trying age for a young lady to be sure. You can imagine after five daughters it is some cause for my mother's nerves."

"I wish my mother was alive to share in the nerves; alas, it falls to me and my cousin as guardians."

"I did not know; I am profusely sorry for your loss." He nodded in acceptance, and she was momentarily lost on what to say. Surprisingly, he began to laugh.

"What is the cause for your merriment?"

He looked at her, eyes twinkling. "I am uncertain I should say."

"Come, I dearly love a laugh."

"I was imagining having five sisters and realised I would either go to an early grave or be the silliest man in the Kingdom. I have heard enough of Bingley's sisters' prattle about fashion. To hear one more mention of lace…"

Elizabeth erupted in laughter, and when she calmed, she gladly shared her amusement. "My father also cannot bear talk of lace. Now you may understand why he is so fond of his library!"

He grinned. "So there might be some hope for me after all? But I do not think your father is always so alone in his library. You are a frequent visitor, are you not?"

"I am fond of reading, and we have enjoyed many healthy debates. I hope, sir, you encourage your sister to read."

"I assure you, Georgiana needs no such encouragement. Although I sometimes must redirect her interests from sentimental novels to weightier topics."

Smiling, Elizabeth replied, "That is as it should be. The elder brother must be the protector of her mind as much as her heart." He seemed pained at her words, and she could only think that mentioning his care for her reminded him of the loss of his parents. "I am sorry; I broach a painful topic, forgive me."

"Do not trouble yourself; all is well. I think, perhaps, my sister might benefit from the influence of well-mannered young ladies nearer her age than her aunts and companion."

"Does she not know Mrs. Hurst and Miss Bingley?" He raised an eyebrow at her, and she nodded. "I see."

"Our acquaintance is very new, but would you give some thought to taking up a correspondence with her?"

"I am flattered, but it hardly seems appropriate without having met her."

He was silent for some minutes, and Elizabeth perceived he was processing many thoughts. "Mr. Darcy?"

"Excuse me, I was thinking too intently. I am uncertain she will desire to visit here, but if I ever have the pleasure of making you two acquainted, I am certain she would be the better for it."

She blushed a little, and by then they had reached the house. Darcy handed his hat full of apples to the butler, and they were shown into the dining-parlour where the others were already gathered.

"Lizzy! Where have you been? And look at you!"

Darcy spoke, "Forgive me, madam, but I found your daughter in need of assistance as I walked the garden."

"Assistance?"

"Mama, it is only a little sprain. I shall rest it after the meal. There is no need to worry about me."

Mrs. Bennet's brow furrowed, and her eyes focused on her daughter.

"Mrs. Bennet, I compliment you on this spread and am most especially looking forward to dessert."

"Oh...well, yes, a special treat to showcase our apples. I always say there is no other place in England where you will find so nice an apple as Hertfordshire."

Elizabeth glanced at Darcy and was pleased to see a light smile on his face. Where she once would have felt mortification, she could only feel amusement at so much they had shared.

*****

March 1812

Rosings Park, Kent

Elizabeth sat under an apple tree along her favourite path at Rosings. The flowers were just beginning to bud, and it would be weeks before the apples came, but she smiled to herself just the same. She would always think of apple trees and her Mr. Darcy. At least she very much wished he was to be her Mr. Darcy.

During the weeks he had spent in Hertfordshire the previous autumn, she grew to admire him greatly. His character was intricate and not easily sketched, one she would be happy to have a lifetime with. Falling from the apple tree began it all, as he was most attentive to her. He and Bingley called several times in the subsequent fortnight. Darcy escorted her around the garden, as she could not walk far, and they always stopped at the apple tree for some moments. Elizabeth learned even more of him when she stayed at Netherfield to assist Jane, who fell ill while visiting.

He could engage her in conversation as no other and treated her opinions as an equal. Once he felt comfortable with his surroundings, he easily conversed and laughed. Their conversations varied from serious to silly. When they first met, he seemed all haughty arrogance, but over time she saw that his reserve and sarcastic wit resembled her own esteemed father's but with greater sense and understanding. Where her father laughed, Darcy gently encouraged. Her mother and sisters would be silly, but perhaps they were not in so much danger as bringing them all to ridicule now.

Eventually, in late November, time came for him to depart Netherfield. They had taken one last walk to the now completely bare apple tree.

"Miss Elizabeth, I hope you know how highly I have come to regard our friendship and how I have enjoyed our walks...and this apple tree. I shall miss...it."

He seemed so nervous that she could only help him along in the way she knew best. "To show how I also value our friendship I pledge that I will only walk to this tree with you. Now you see, you will have to return to Netherfield before too long, or I shall be forced to shun a portion of my own garden!"

He smiled weakly and squeezed the hand that rested on his arm. "I wish I may, I wish I may."

Several weeks passed before he returned, and then it was on the happy occasion of Jane and Bingley's wedding. He brought Miss Darcy with him. Although shy at first, Elizabeth and Georgiana were soon fast friends. The Darcys returned to Town after the wedding breakfast, and Elizabeth had no time for private conversation with Mr. Darcy. However, she and Georgiana eagerly began a correspondence.

Darcy visited again a few weeks later. On a warm February day, she told Darcy of meeting Mr. George Wickham, a new lieutenant in the militia stationed in Meryton, just after Darcy left the area in November. Upon hearing Mr. Darcy of Pemberley had come to Bingley's wedding, Mr. Wickham blamed Darcy as the cause of his poverty. Elizabeth could not believe his words.

Darcy's eyes flashed in anger, but he told her the truth of his history with the reprobate, including Wickham's designs on Georgiana. After the emotional turmoil had passed, he looked at her intently.

"You were walking in the garden when he spoke of me?"

"Yes."

Very quietly, he asked, "May I ask where in the garden you were walking?"

"By the wilderness." She could not understand why he was so concerned over the location of the conversation.

His eyes closed in relief. "So you did not walk to *our*, this, tree?"

Blushing and averting her eyes, she shook her head. "No, sir. I keep my pledges."

Her heart began to beat faster, and she heard him take in a quick breath.

Stealing a look at him, she was entranced by what she saw and hardly knew what to hope for next.

"As do I, Miss Bennet."

She held her breath waiting for him to say more, but he turned them back to the house. After speaking with her father about Wickham, Darcy departed the next day. She knew he was well, though he was very busy with some financial investments, due to her correspondence with his sister, but it could not take the place of seeing him.

Now she was in Kent visiting Mrs. Collins, her newly married friend. Mr. Collins, aside from being Elizabeth's cousin and her father's heir, was the rector for a very great lady who happened to be Darcy's aunt. He arrived yesterday and immediately called on the parsonage, but Elizabeth desperately wished they might walk together once more.

*****

Darcy stormed out of the big house. He had just done battle with his aunt, who refused to accept his statements that he would not marry his cousin. Anne, of course, had always been in complete agreement with him and attempted to explain to her mother, but the lady would think as she wished. He shook his head. At the moment, he wished to have only one thought, of the one who had been at the centre of most of his since a lovely day in October. *Elizabeth.*

He intended to walk to the parsonage but found her sitting under a newly blooming tree near the lane he favoured. Her eyes were closed, and she did not hear his approach.

"Elizabeth?"

She sighed. "Fitzwilliam." Darcy thought he would have to kiss her right there. She seemed to suddenly realise this was not a dream, and her eyes flew open even as she coloured. "Mr. Darcy!"

He sat down beside her. "I find you under an apple tree instead of atop of one."

She laughed, and he grinned. Her laughter ceased when she looked discerningly at his face. "You look tired. Was your journey yesterday so unbearable?"

"No, what is twenty miles of good road? It is my aunt who is unbearable."

She would not reply but suppressed a smile.

"I always knew she would not take my news well, and that is why I have put it off as long as I have. I told you once I keep my promises. This particular one does not bring me much joy, but I must follow my duty."

"What is your dreadful news? Scottish highlanders have besieged your estate?"

He chuckled. "In her opinion, my news is infinitely worse. I informed her that I have decided to take a wife."

Elizabeth paled and coloured all at once, and he hardly knew what to say or do next, but she always rose to any occasion.

"And do you have a woman in mind already?"

"Oh yes. She was formed for me, I would say." He found it hard to look at her and not kiss her. Instead, he studied the path for a minute. When she did not reply, he glanced over at her; she seemed deeply troubled. "This makes you unhappy?"

"Oh, of course not! I only do not understand why it would displease your aunt." Was it his imagination or were tears threatening her eyes?

"She is a foolish woman and believes she can order me about, but I have made my choice."

Unexpectedly, Elizabeth stood. "Forgive me, Charlotte will wonder where I am."

"May I escort you back?"

She did not give an immediate reply but finally nodded. He offered her his arm, and she hesitated.

"Come, what is this? It is not like my dear friend to be melancholy."

"You must forgive me. I have a sudden headache."

They had not moved. "May I walk with you tomorrow?"

In an instant, Elizabeth snatched her arm from his, and her eyes flashed. "How dare you? No, I am finished saving my walks for you!"

"What?"

"You made it perfectly clear you have made your choice, and now I have made mine!"

She spun around and took but a few steps before he caught her hand and turned her to face him.

"Good God! What is the matter?" She held his eyes, and her fury was evident. "Dearest Elizabeth, tell me. What have I done to anger you?"

"You have gone and proposed...what did you call me?"

"Proposed?"

Elizabeth trembled, and Darcy pulled her closer to him. "I assure you, I have not proposed yet."

"Yet?"

"I believe you will be the first to know when I have."

"Yes, I suppose Georgiana would tell me."

"I had rather thought you would tell her."

"You ask too much!"

Still not understanding her anger but growing desperate, he stepped even closer. "I have not yet asked for enough. I have not yet asked for your hand or your heart."

Elizabeth blinked rapidly before breaking into a beautiful smile.

"My loveliest Elizabeth, I have adored you and ardently loved you these many months past. I waited only so long as to take care of some business and announce my intentions to my aunt, although my cousin and I have always been in agreement on the matter. You must know, surely you must know, you have had my heart since you fell from that apple tree, and now I only wish to know yours. You taught me to think beyond myself, beyond my concerns, and to the cares of others. That day I offered you my hand; today I ask for yours."

"Yes!" she replied without hesitation. "Yes, you may have my hand for you have held my heart for so long."

*****

Their happiness could not be contained to smiles alone, and after kisses replaced their laughter, Darcy had but a few questions.

"How could you believe I was offering for another?"

"I believed you meant your cousin. As you say, your aunt is very much in favour of the match."

"She said it to you?" It was beyond belief.

"She hinted very strongly, but it was...Mr. Wickham," she finished very lowly.

"That rat! If he knew I had been at Netherfield, then he must have heard of our friendship and only meant to put you off."

"You are not angry that I believed him?"

"You could not have been so angry with me if you had really believed him. I doubt you thought there was truth of it at all until I made you doubt me. Will you forgive me? I ought to have spoken to you in February or even earlier." He could not look at her, thinking of the sorrow she must have felt due to him.

"Fitzwilliam." He looked up sharply as she said his name and squeezed his hands. "It was but a moment of fear. I scarcely hoped before, but neither did I doubt you. Now that you have given me your heart to protect, I will never doubt again."

"But why should my aunt be unhappy then if I wished to marry Anne?"

"It is so very silly, but my mind had to conjure something. I assumed you desired to send her to the Dower House, and she was angry."

"Would I send my mother-in-law to the Dower House?"

"Not even you can be so angelic!"

"Perhaps not for my aunt, but your family will always be welcome with us."

"How did I ever think you proud?"

"I was arrogant. I was selfish. I thought of my own comfort. And while I told myself I was always perfectly rational and allowed behaviour to be my guide in my associations, I did make too many allowances for rank and fortune. In October, I would have believed my aunt superior to your mother. But what cause has Lady Catherine to worry or treat people poorly? Such a lesson I learned through you!"

Darcy had no more words for his feelings but was most effective at displaying them. Their kisses ceased when Elizabeth broke into laughter.

"What? What is it?" Darcy asked.

"I was only wondering if Pemberley had any apple trees for me to climb."

"Dozens, my dear, but we may plant more if you wish. I only ask they not be of the sour kind you have at Longbourn!"

Recalling her thoughts that day and the expression he had as he tasted the sour fruit, Elizabeth could only laugh more and vow to herself to never allow Darcy another unpleasant expression or thought again. She would keep the promise.

There the roots that nourished a strong love for weathering the trials of life were formed, under the apple tree.

The End

Tolerable Feelings

I have written quite a few forced marriage stories for Darcy and Elizabeth, but what would happen to them if Jane and Bingley were the couple forced to wed?

Early October 1811

Meryton, Hertfordshire

Elizabeth Bennet awoke the morning after the Meryton Assembly expecting some sign that the world as she knew it had come to an utter end. Instead, she was met with glorious sunshine and the beaming face of her sister.

"Did I wake you, Lizzy?"

Elizabeth yawned and stretched. "No."

Jane smiled again. "I can hardly believe this has happened. And why must I giggle so? I feel as though I am Lydia!"

Elizabeth looked at her eldest and dearest sister in confusion. If she did not know her sister to be perfectly well and had not seen the events of last night with her own eyes, she might fear her sister ill. Her sister was compromised during the dance and would be entering into a marriage with a total stranger. For any other young lady, there might be hope that her reputation would not be smeared by such an obvious accident, and in plain view of so many witnesses. However, Mrs. Bennet would never allow an opportunity to marry off one of her daughters to pass by and so she escalated the situation.

Mr. Bingley was a nice enough man, but who could want to marry a man off of one night's acquaintance? Her sister, apparently. Elizabeth firmly believed in first impressions, but not love at first sight! Other memories from the night before tried to encroach. His friend had haughtily refused to dance with any of the ladies from the neighbourhood. When Elizabeth was specifically pointed out as a possible dance partner, Mr. Darcy coldly declared her "Tolerable but not handsome enough" and then claimed she sat out because she was slighted by other men when in truth there was a shortage of men at the ball!

Pushing the thoughts aside, Elizabeth glanced towards the hook on their wall where Jane's ball gown was stored, as if on display, until it could be mended.

Suddenly the door to their room burst open, and Mrs. Bennet's shrill voice broke out. "Make haste, Jane! Make haste! He has come!"

Elizabeth was too tired to understand. "Who has come?"

"Mr. Bingley, of course! He has four or five thousand a year and likely more! Oh, I knew you could not be so beautiful for nothing my dear, dear child! Of course, having him step on your dress and rip it seems more like one of Lizzy's clever designs, but to be sure, he was entirely bewitched by you. Here is Sarah to help you along! Make haste!"

Elizabeth could only bat her eyes in disbelief after her mother left. She readied herself quickly; the poor man should have some sensible conversation while Jane was put through the full rigours of a toilette. Upon entering the drawing room, her eyes locked on the image of one person she hoped never to meet again.

I truly hope he is not very close friends with the man that is to be my brother.

Mr. Bingley was nowhere to be seen, and Elizabeth surmised that he must be in conference with her father. Why his friend, Mr. Darcy, needed to come on a call that settled a marriage Elizabeth knew not. Her youngest sisters were still abed, and her middle sister, Mary, was abusing the pianoforte in the other parlour.

At Elizabeth's entrance, Mr. Darcy stood and bowed in perfect, if cold, civility, but Elizabeth dared not believe the pretence. He was the rudest man she had ever met. Mrs. Bennet was all happiness at Elizabeth's presence and quickly excused herself on some matter.

Elizabeth suppressed a groan. Although the door was left open, it was not entirely proper for her to be left alone with the gentleman. A quick glance at Mr. Darcy confirmed that he was conscious of the concern as well.

Suppressing her indignation at her mother's behaviour, Elizabeth spoke to her guest. "Are you well, Mr. Darcy?"

"Perfectly tolerable." Elizabeth smirked. He certainly liked the word. There was a silence, and he fidgeted a bit too much before he was roused to return the civility.

"Oh, I am tolerable, I suppose." Elizabeth cast a mocking look at him and was surprised to see a hint of a smile on his face. "Could I tempt you to join us at breakfast? Or are you more in humour for tea and light refreshments?" Despite what seemed to be a valiant effort, Darcy's smile widened a fraction.

"Thank you, but I am perfectly content just now."

Elizabeth soon heard Bingley in the hall. Believing the two gentlemen may desire a private conversation, she stood and made to leave. Looking over her shoulder, she called back, "I will let your friend return to you, and you may enjoy his smiles, for you would be wasting your time with me." As she left, she heard a light chuckle.

*****

Mid-October 1811

Hertfordshire

Darcy entered Lucas Lodge with a feeling of anticipation. He could not quite remember the last time he felt such. His holiday at his dearest friend's leased estate was proving to be quite unexpected in more ways than one. Bingley had accidentally compromised a young lady and proposed nearly a minute later. It might have been wise to see if her reputation was harmed first!

Darcy intended to meet the woman's family, to support his friend if need be. He fully expected a nest of vipers and fortune hunters given how fast they all agreed to the engagement. Instead, he was teased by an enchanting and quick-witted young lady, the very one he had insulted the night before. Somehow after that encounter, the shrill voice of the mother and silliness of the youngest sisters mattered little.

He had been in Miss Elizabeth's company for four more evenings and nearly daily visits to Longbourn in the last fortnight and found her more bewitching with each conversation. He was wrong to dismiss her as only tolerable at first sight. She was quite pretty, and her eyes were very fine. Her figure was light and pleasing, her manners catching and playful. He could scarcely stay away from her.

He enjoyed their conversations very much. In an environment where he knew no one but was sought after, and already melancholy over trouble with his sister, he was grateful for a friend. Which put to mind the reason for his anticipation this evening, or at least what he told himself was the reason for his anticipation.

Darcy watched Elizabeth all night, wondering when he might say his piece to her. She perceived his staring and eavesdropping and teased him for it. When she sang that evening, an odd feeling settled in his chest. As some of the other young people rolled up the rug to begin dancing, Darcy was only too happy to oblige when Sir William Lucas suggested Elizabeth as a dance partner, although she initially refused.

"Will you dance, Miss Elizabeth?" he asked with more sincerity than he ever felt before. The pounding of his heart was surely because of the conversation he intended to have for his sister's sake.

Her brow furrowed, but she conceded. "Very well." Darcy ignored the ridiculous feeling of triumph.

Before they could even begin, Sir William was gloating. "I hope to have this scene often repeated once a certain desirable event takes place. Capital!" He glanced at Jane and Bingley dancing, and so did Darcy and Elizabeth. The movements of the dance led them away from Sir William. Elizabeth cast worried looks at her sister.

"What troubles you?" Darcy inquired.

"I worry for their happiness."

"You do not believe in love at first sight?"

"We all might begin freely—a slight preference is natural enough. But real love needs to be nurtured, and that cannot happen in one night, or even a fortnight."

"There are still many weeks before the wedding." Elizabeth nodded in sad acquiescence. "I am happy to hear you do not stand by first impressions only. I can remember some expressions I have said that might justly make you hate me."

"Are you accusing me of a propensity to hate everyone?"

"No, only to willfully misunderstand."

"And you believe I have misunderstood you? Did I misunderstand your desire to resist dancing your first night in the neighbourhood? Or have I misunderstood your poor opinion of all of us and refusal to treat us as equals and socialise?"

Darcy was ashamed of his actions but hoped to ease the affront he caused. "I do not have the habit of conversing easily with those I have never met before."

Elizabeth merely pursed her lips and replied, "What a tolerable dancing partner you are."

Darcy smiled for a moment before beginning again. "Only when my partner is lively and enchanting." He smiled at her blush and directed the conversation to the topic he desired. "Bingley tells me he and your sister have issued an invitation for you to spend the winter with them in Town."

"Yes, but I am uncertain I wish to intrude on their privacy." They passed Mrs. Bennet, who was loudly extolling how Jane could now throw her sisters in the path of other rich men. Elizabeth visibly cringed.

"If you do visit I was hoping I might introduce my sister to you." His words clearly caught Elizabeth by surprise, and she stumbled a little. Darcy reached to steady her. "I believe she could benefit from your liveliness and intelligence."

"I would be honoured to meet her." Darcy expected to feel satisfaction at her favourable reply but instead only felt more anticipation.

*****

November 26, 1811

Netherfield Park, Hertfordshire

"Mr. Darcy! Miss Eliza, excuse me, Miss Bennet, I must see you dance tonight!" Sir William spoke as though he had been liberally sampling the punch at the ball given in honour of Jane and Bingley's wedding.

Elizabeth was of a mind to refuse. She could hardly bear parting with Jane on this day.

Darcy's gentle voice broke through her thoughts. "Will you dance, Miss Bennet?"

She looked up in surprise at Darcy, though she knew not why. She had let go of her first impressions of him and found him enjoyable company but continually discovered a new facet of his character. He often seemed silent when others were given to merriment, and yet he could be verbose at the least expected moments, animated on the least likely topics.

She allowed Darcy to lead her to the dance floor. "I suppose I ought to become accustomed to always being Miss Bennet now."

Sir William called after them, "Capital! I hope to see this often repeated!"

Elizabeth let out an exasperated sigh. "I wonder how he thinks we might frequently dance together. You have your own estate to run and cannot constantly be visiting your friend's, and Jane and Bingley mean to leave for Town after Christmas."

She could not quite understand the disappointment she felt at not seeing Darcy as often.

Darcy gave her a sympathetic look. "Are you still determined to remain at Longbourn then?"

They rounded a loud Mrs. Bennet, who in addition to crowing about Jane's marriage, now declared that Elizabeth would be the next mistress of Longbourn. Elizabeth glanced to her cousin and father's heir, the ridiculous Mr. Collins, and cringed. She nearly stepped on Darcy's toes.

"I must admit Town does have more of an appeal to me at present than several weeks ago."

Darcy smiled. "My sister greatly looks forward to meeting you."

Elizabeth affected an amused tone. "I hope to prove to be a tolerable friend then."

Shaking his head while smiling, Darcy replied, "You are a very agreeable friend. You express yourself uncommonly well and always with great energy."

His words cheered her but she was in little humour to enjoy the day beyond hoping her sister's smiles were genuine, and her new brother would always seek to please his wife.

*****

March 2, 1812

Bingley residence, London

"Eliza! Are you certain you must leave Town on the morrow to spend so much time in Kent? You will be missing much of the Season, and Colonel Brandon seems quite taken with you!"

Elizabeth quelled the urge to roll her eyes at Caroline. They had both been staying with the Bingleys for several months, and Caroline assumed a false closeness with her. "I will be very happy to visit my friend and enjoy all Kent has to offer. I am certain Colonel Brandon will find other agreeable company."

Caroline tsked. "Always so imprudent. First rejecting the parson, resulting in your mother's insistence in your *banishment* from your family home, and now spurning a wealthy and agreeable suitor."

"He is hardly a suitor. Mere dances are not the same as paying court."

Instead of replying, Caroline declared a desire to perform on the pianoforte. After she left, Darcy took her place and spoke with Elizabeth.

"Did you enjoy the evening?" They had just returned from a ball in Town and now were having a light supper at Jane and Bingley's house.

"It was certainly tolerable." Darcy grinned, and Elizabeth smiled at the sight. She could not understand why he was never provoked by her teasing but was pleased she could always humour him.

"Do you truly look forward to your holiday in Kent?" He studied his hands before adding, "Or do you only desire a change in companionship?"

Elizabeth sighed. "I do miss Charlotte, and I am always curious to see more of the world. As for my London companions, I find them all excessively agreeable, save one. I do not know why she dislikes me so!"

They both looked towards Caroline, who narrowed her sharp eyes at them. "Perhaps she is jealous of certain friendships you have established."

"A friendship is hardly the sort of thing Caroline is likely to be jealous over."

"*Certain* friendships easily inspire jealousy," he said gravely, and when Elizabeth turned to see his face, she was surprised to see an unmistakable look of admiration in his eyes.

She said nothing as her heart beat faster. Surely he could not be implying he cared for her! Why, they had been friends for months now, and he never said a thing!

Before she could gather her wits, Darcy spoke. "How long will you be at Hunsford?"

"I am to remain six weeks."

Darcy grinned. "I have recently had a letter from my aunt and conferred with my cousin. We are to visit her for Easter."

Elizabeth smiled. Darcy's presence would be an agreeable addition to what otherwise would likely be mostly ridiculous company. They moved to the coffee table to refill their cups.

"My sister will miss your friendship in *your* absence." She reached for his cup, and his hand lingered on hers for a moment. "May I hope you will miss *certain* friendships as well?"

Elizabeth could hardly breathe. He removed his hand, but hers now felt afire. Dropping her eyes, she managed to reply, "Yes, I will."

She heard a quick intake of breath and gathered courage to look at him. Although he tried to hide it, she easily noticed his smile. "I wish you a very enjoyable stay then."

Before Elizabeth could make sense of why the candles all seemed to burn brighter, the music sounded sweeter, and all the company more enjoyable, Darcy was making his apologies to his hosts. Unaware of her eagerness to catch one last glimpse of him, her eyes locked with his before he left with a slight smile on his face.

*****

March 30, 1812

Hunsford Parsonage, Kent

Elizabeth glanced up from a letter from Jane, which shared her news of expected joy arriving in September, when she heard the bell alerting her to a visitor.

"Mr. Darcy! I had not expected you, sir."

He gave her a confused look. "You did not think I would call on the parsonage again?"

Elizabeth blushed. "You have not returned in the last week. I had thought..."

She had tried to laugh herself out of it. These things happen often enough. Young men often believed themselves in love until accident separates the couple. He had visited the day after his arrival in Kent, which she believed was sign of his continued regard but as he had not come since, she was left to believe his admiration ceased. She knew of his family's hopes that he would marry his cousin. If only she had not persuaded herself of such a strong attachment to him!

Darcy had walked closer while she was unaware. "I regret I was very busy helping my cousin, Anne, settle affairs."

How could he say the words with such calmness and gentleness when it felt as though a knife were stabbed into her heart?

"What happy news." She tried to smile.

"Yes, she has recently gained her majority and is now the rightful owner of Rosings estate."

Tears slipped from Elizabeth's eyes as she considered her foolishness. Why would Darcy want her when he could have any wealthy, beautiful, and accomplished lady?

Seeing her tears and then the letter in her hand, Darcy cried out in alarm. "Good God! What is the matter? Is it news from London? From Longbourn?"

Elizabeth looked up in confusion, and when she trembled, Darcy led her to a chair. "Let me call your maid. Is there nothing you could take to give you present relief? A glass of wine; shall I get you one? You are very ill."

"No, I thank you," she replied, endeavouring to recover herself. "There is nothing the matter with me. I am quite well; I am only..."

She burst into tears as she attempted to explain some reason for her distress. For a few minutes, she could not speak another word. Darcy, in wretched suspense, could only say something indistinctly of his concern and observe her in compassionate silence. At length, he took the letter from her hands and scanned the contents.

"I see nothing alarming in here. There is reason for great joy."

Grateful she might have a cause to explain her outburst, she nodded. "Oh yes. I am unbelievably happy for them both."

"You have determined first impressions were correct after all then?" he asked in a tone that was clearly meant to make her smile but failed in his object.

"Oh no. I have quite learned not to rely on them. You have turned out entirely different than I first suspected, and your information on Mr. Wickham was contrary to his charming façade."

"You still believe time is needed to nurture an acquaintance?" She nodded. "To nurture love?"

Tears threatened to spill again, but she determinedly met Darcy's eyes. "Yes."

"We have been acquainted quite some time now, have we not?"

"Above six months, I believe."

"I have endeavoured to be a patient man, Elizabeth. But I am selfish as well. I can go no longer without telling you how much I admire and love you."

At such words, she cried again, and Darcy knelt before her. "If your earlier tears were for happiness at your sister's news, then may I hope my words bring you joy as well?"

Not trusting herself to speak, Elizabeth only nodded.

"Then your feelings of me have changed since we first met? Do you like me now?"

Blushing scarlet as he referenced her first prejudiced opinions of him, she forced herself to speak. "Perhaps I did not always like you as well as I do now, but I do like you! I love you!"

Heartfelt delight diffused over his face. "Dearest, loveliest Elizabeth! Dare I hope you will consent to be my wife?"

Elizabeth grinned and then pursed her lips in a mischievous manner. "I find you are quite tolerable enough to tempt me to matrimony."

After Darcy returned the favour of her teasing in the manner he had long wished, by adoring her lips with his own, she desired to only provoke him again. "How did you begin to love me?"

"I was in the middle before I knew I had begun."

"You admired me for my impertinence, did you not? Or was it after I came to London, and you discovered I was not slighted by other men after all?"

Darcy let out a laugh. "Must you remember my words from that night so perfectly?"

"I believe it belongs to me to find occasions for teasing and quarrelling with you as often as may be. In return, my good qualities fall to your protection, and you may exaggerate them as much as possible. To be sure, there is little actual good in me."

"There is plenty of good in your affectionate behaviour to both Jane and Georgiana."

"Who can do less for them? But why did you not visit again earlier?"

"Lady Catherine will be displeased by our engagement. Matters with Anne have been settled in such a way that my aunt must behave or be removed from the house."

"Indeed!" Elizabeth tried to hide her amusement in imagining such a scene. "But why did you not speak of your feelings earlier?"

"I was embarrassed by your first opinion of me and can only say a man who felt less might have said earlier."

Such a statement of regard could only be rewarded with more kisses until the Collinses returned. Lady Catherine was very upset at news of the betrothal but moderated her anger when her daughter proved she was prepared to do battle. Darcy soon sought Mr. Bennet's blessing, and the couple were united in matrimony in June. After a blissful summer at the Lakes and Pemberley, they settled into their lives that were much more than tolerable. Indeed, their lives were filled with such happiness and good humour that all of their dearest family and friends smiled in return.

The End

Rose Fairbanks

Compassion for Me

What would happen if Mr. Bingley had actually sprained his ankle at the Meryton Assembly?

"If he had had any compassion for me," cried her husband impatiently, "he would not have danced half so much! For God's sake, say no more of his partners. O that he had sprained his ankle in the first dance!"

— *Pride and Prejudice*, Chapter 3

"Do you enjoy dancing, Mr. Bingley?"

Charlotte Lucas could not have been more pleased to be asked to dance the first set by the handsome newcomer to their little end of Hertfordshire. She knew it was only out of deference to her father's position as a knight and host of this evening's events, but Charlotte was flattered just the same. At seven and twenty, and with a shortage of gentlemen in the neighbourhood, she seldom danced at the balls any longer. She knew she was rather plain and felt his compassion as he seemed to genuinely enjoy dancing with her, instead of merely tolerating the experience as others had done.

Mr. Bingley was a very amiable sort of gentleman; or at least he had been until they went down the set the first time, and his eyes found her friend, Jane Bennet.

"Mr. Bingley?"

"Forgive me. You were saying."

Charlotte suppressed a grin as the dance separated them. Most men were taken with Jane's beauty, and while Charlotte could be jealous if she wished, she would rather be happy if her friend finally had a suitor of independent means...and who could withstand her family's...eccentricities. Of course, Mr. Bingley was not a landed gentleman; he had no cause to be so proud like the other men who fell at Jane's altar. Not that it would hurt a thing for her to be more encouraging.

When the steps to the dance allowed her to speak once more, she tried again. "I had asked if you enjoy dancing."

"Oh, very much! I intend to dance every set, although I have not been introduced to any of the other ladies yet."

This was no surprise. She knew for a fact that he had not so much as glimpsed the Bennet sisters before tonight, much to their extreme displeasure. Naturally, Mrs. Bennet claimed him for one of her own as soon as she heard his income. It did not matter a thing about his character or even if he was handsome. Truthfully, Charlotte quite agreed with her. With a large enough income, a woman could bear almost anything.

"I would be happy to introduce you to any lady who strikes your fancy."

He beamed. "In that case, I would very much like an introduction with the angel over there in blue..."

Mr. Bingley did not finish his statement, for he landed oddly on his right foot, instantly paled in pain, and staggered off the dance floor. Thankfully it was crowded enough that none of the more intrusive members of Meryton society noticed them leave the floor.

"Mr. Bingley! Are you well?"

"I believe I have sprained my ankle."

"Oh my! Allow me to fetch my father."

She left Mr. Bingley leaning against a wall as there were no seats to be had. She could not find her father but located her brother and explained the situation. He would search for their father while she was to return to Mr. Bingley. As she approached, she noticed that Mr. Bingley's friend, Mr. Darcy, was now with him.

"Come, Darcy. I will have to leave, but will you stay? I should hate for our whole party to leave when I am so new in the neighbourhood."

"Surely they will understand."

Mr. Bingley pulled Mr. Darcy in closer, but Charlotte always had very acute hearing. "Miss Lucas was about to introduce me to the most beautiful lady I have ever beheld. An angel! I cannot bear for her to think ill of me. Would you dance with her and tell her of me?"

"Bingley!"

"You will have to dance with others as well. Several of the ladies here are uncommonly pretty. There must be someone to meet your fastidious standards. But you must dance! If not, they will think the whole party hateful and arrogant. Please?"

Charlotte had to hide a chuckle at Mr. Bingley's pleading look.

"Very well, but only because I do not wish to offend your neighbours."

"I knew you would have compassion for me."

"You realise my main motivation is so we will have engagements to attend as often as possible, and I may be away from your sisters?"

Mr. Bingley laughed, and Mr. Darcy smiled. Bingley looked over Mr. Darcy's shoulder, finally noticing Charlotte just as her father and brother arrived.

"Ah, Miss Lucas. You have returned with your father and your brother, I see."

"I thought they might assist you. I took the liberty to call your carriage."

"Thank you." With one man clutching each arm, Bingley managed to leave the ballroom. Charlotte was left to stand with Mr. Darcy.

"Do you dance, Mr. Darcy?"

He chuckled while shaking his head. "I do tonight. I cannot tell you how many times Bingley has dragged me to a ball and stayed the whole night. I have often wished he sprained his ankle in the first set so we might leave early, and now I am to be his image in the neighbourhood in his absence!"

He took a deep breath. "I would be most pleased to finish Bingley's set with you, Miss Lucas."

Charlotte smiled as an idea formed in her mind, and she happily accepted his request.

After some silence, Charlotte decided to assist matters. "Your friend had asked for an introduction to the eldest Miss Bennet."

"Ah, yes. His angel." He rolled his eyes.

"Do I understand you wish to meet more partners?"

Letting out an exasperated sigh, Mr. Darcy agreed. "I do tonight."

"Forgive me, but I could not help but hear you have fastidious standards. Which do you prefer, blonde or brunette? Tall like you or short?"

Mr. Darcy looked at her with a touch of disgust until he saw her sly smile. "Truthfully, beauty matters little, especially in a ballroom. I dislike dancing, and I cannot recommend myself to strangers. My standards are only pleasant conversation." He shrewdly examined her. "Might you have any friends who are as witty and clever as you?"

"I do, indeed. One enjoys teasing very much as well." Mr. Darcy frowned a little, and Charlotte added, "But I will tell you some stories that you may use to your advantage, and I assure you, she is quite pretty."

"Which lady do you mean?"

Charlotte waited for them to pass by her friends. "Mr. Bingley's angel is in blue, but my clever friend is in green."

The rest of the set passed in pleasant conversation, although Mr. Darcy frequently seemed distracted as they passed a certain lady, and when they finished, Charlotte introduced him to two of the Bennet sisters.

"Mr. Darcy, this is the eldest Miss Bennet, and here is my good friend, Miss Elizabeth Bennet."

Charlotte was pleased to see Darcy give Elizabeth a genuine smile as Jane's partner came to collect her for the next dance. "If you are not otherwise engaged for the next set, might I have the honour, Miss Elizabeth?"

After her friend's acceptance, Mr. Darcy began to lead her to the dance floor. Charlotte was happy to overhear him say, with an obvious smile on his face, "I have been wondering if you knew of any fine trees to climb..."

*****

Six weeks later

Charlotte and Elizabeth stood in an alcove at the ball at Netherfield, held in honour of the engagements of the eldest two

Miss Bennets to the single Netherfield gentlemen.

"Charlotte, you never did tell me what made you think Fitzwilliam would enjoy a dance with me."

"Oh, it was when he confessed to desiring Bingley to sprain his ankle in the first set on every other occasion. I could only think how much it sounded like something your father would say, and I know you enjoy his wit."

"What a strange friend you are! I really should be more vexed that you have no compassion for me and will spill the secrets of my childhood exploits to just any stranger who happens upon you!"

Elizabeth and Charlotte laughed before hugging. Darcy and an army officer approached. "My dear friend, Miss Charlotte Lucas," Darcy said, "allow me to introduce my cousin, Colonel Jonathan Fitzwilliam."

After the usual civilities, the two moved to the dance floor. Darcy and Elizabeth overheard the colonel say, "I regret that I am not a naval captain, Miss

Lucas, for I have heard you are infinitely fond of them..."

Charlotte shot a withering glare at Elizabeth as the colonel laughed and tugged her hand.

"An excellent idea, my love," Darcy said to Elizabeth.

"Well, now it is *her* turn to be teased!"

The End

An Ungentlemanly Manner

I've always wondered what would have happened if Darcy reacted to Elizabeth's claims of him being ungentlemanly. This was my very first completed Pride and Prejudice story and I posted it on an online fan fiction forum.

"You are mistaken, Mr. Darcy, if you suppose that the mode of your declaration affected me in any other way, than as it spared me the concern which I might have felt in refusing you, had you behaved in a more gentlemanlike manner."

She saw him start at this, but he said nothing, and she continued: "You could not have made the offer of your hand in any possible way that would have tempted me to accept it."

–Pride and Prejudice, Chapter 34

"....had you behaved in a more gentlemanlike manner."

And just like that, seven and twenty years of education and good breeding disappeared from Mr. Darcy's mind. *If she will accuse me of being ungentlemanly, I will show her conduct that is truly ungentlemanly!*

Darcy stepped forward with a decided air before she could continue her rantings. "You accuse me of ungentlemanly conduct towards yourself? I see you prefer the gallant, like Mr. Wickham, perhaps? So, should I have approached you at the impressionable and young age of fifteen while on a holiday without your elder brother—your only surviving family and your guardian—and convinced you of an elopement? When confronted by said brother by the merest chance of arrival before the event could take place, and it was made clear that I would not receive any of your substantial dowry of thirty thousand pounds, should I have announced that you were not worth the marriage otherwise and left you grieving and brokenhearted, so much so that almost a twelvemonth later and you are still painfully unsure of yourself and decisions, certain that your every action will be the ruin of your family? All your joy and liveliness vanished? So much that you are merely a walking ghost in your homes, leaving your brother to grieve as though the last member of his family has passed?"

He saw her begin to shrink back from his claims, but still he ungentlemanly pushed forward, regardless of her sensibilities. She was speechless, and he would not give her a moment to collect her thoughts.

"Or should I have flattered you and seduced you until you begged for me to take your virtue, only to abandon you and leave you with child like most servants and tradesmen's daughters and even a few gentlewomen unfortunate enough to cross his path?

"Or do you prefer my cousin? I should flirt shamelessly and raise your expectations all the while knowing that I must marry a well-dowered woman to continue married life in my preferred lifestyle? It would be great love indeed that would make him overlook such things." Elizabeth had turned pale at his information about Mr. Wickham but now blushed. Darcy would wager his cousin had said something of the effect to her.

"Shall I evaluate Mr. Collins? Tell me, in his proposal to either you or Mrs. Collins, how many utterances fell from his tongue on the greatness of my aunt?" Elizabeth's eyes widened in confusion and disbelief, so Darcy clarified what he knew. "Oh yes, I know of his proposal to you as he did not keep it a secret from my aunt! Of course, his version could hardly be the truth. He claims you rescinded your acceptance of his suit after realising how ill-suited you are to be the wife of a minister. Did he expect for you to grovel to her and cater to her whims as well as he?

"Do you believe Mr. Bingley is the epitome of gentlemanly behaviour?" Instead of Elizabeth's usual impudent confidence, she looked uncertain. He knew she had believed Bingley far more gentlemanly than him, but he would not allow her to lay Bingley's defection of Miss Bennet all at his door. "Bingley's attachment of only a few weeks must be no deeper than any other time he has supposedly fallen in love, as testament to his agreement to abandon the acquaintance when pressured by his sisters concerning the prudence of the match and my uncertainty regarding the lady in question's affections.

"Yes, I can see how any of these actions would be much more gentlemanly than for me to declare my ardent love for you despite the objections I shall face from my family and society. A love that has been strong enough to overcome the differences in our station and take on the lower connections of your family and yoke myself to their most improper behaviour—all while receiving no great sign of your regard. Yet I could not leave without paying you my addresses, certain as I am that fate threw us together again." Elizabeth had been looking at her feet, but her eyes met his with his final statement.

"And yet, I will show you *my* ungentlemanly manner now. I will tell you that by our third meeting I was more bewitched by you than any other woman of my acquaintance. Your eyes were the first to strike me, followed by your pleasing form. As I moved from staring at you across the room to listening to your conversations, I discovered your playful manners, intelligence, and quick wit."

He took a step forward, but Elizabeth did not move backwards. "Shall I tell you how disappointed I was when you denied me a dance, not once but twice? Me! No other woman would ever dream of denying me a thing. Shall I describe the jealousy I experienced each moment you danced with another at the Netherfield Ball? That I can recall each time I have seen you bestow a smile on any and all others but me? Should I tell you that I saw your friendship with Miss Lucas? That while you were affectionately nursing your sister, I desired my own sister to have the same claim on you? That I see an inner strength and beauty in you when you would overcome Miss Bingley, and even Lady Catherine's, belittling words? That you are the most genuine and unaffected woman I have ever met?"

She looked at him as though she were seeing him for the first time. Perhaps other men would have described their lady's beautiful face, but he needed Elizabeth to comprehend that it was her character and spirit that had captivated him. As she remained silent, he decided to tell her the extent of his truly ungentlemanly thoughts. "Or shall I tell you that the image of you arriving at Netherfield, flushed and windblown, was so captivating that it will stay in my memory for eternity? In light of you rejecting my suit, I pray to God that is the last image I see in my mind's eye before departing this earth, although my imagination has created much more tempting images. Shall I tell you that I know the room you stayed in at Netherfield was seven paces from my door? That so intoxicating is your scent that I have ordered lavender bushes to be planted outside my study window at Pemberley and even acquired a jar of lavender oil to remind me of your fragrance? Or can I convince you to accept me if I admit that I, a very private man, have laid out my faults bare to you like none other, and instead of feeling indignation, only feel more love inspired by each reproof?

"And there is one fault I have not admitted to as of yet, though I am certain you have deduced it. I am unbelievably obstinate and will do everything in my power to get my way." He stepped even closer to Elizabeth and gently stroked her cheek. She took in a startled breath but did not move or look to be unwelcoming.

"And now I will tell you the ungentlemanly ways I have imagined the feel of your soft skin...so soft, and how your silken strands would feel in my hands." He undid several of Elizabeth's hair pins and ran his fingers through her delightful curls.

"Your lush ruby lips on mine," he leaned in and gave her the lightest of kisses. She gasped, her breathing turned heavy.

"I will tell you how I have imagined your breathing ragged for me, you trembling for my embrace." Seeing her doing thus, he pulled her in his arms, nestling his head above hers. The exquisite feeling of home he experienced nearly overshadowed the desire he felt as her soft body moulded to his.

Stroking her back lightly, he murmured in her hair, "I will tell you how I wish to see your eyes drunk with desire for me. In my imaginings, I have held you in my arms all night long, every night since the fourteenth of October. I have a passion for you that would make me give away Pemberley itself, lay aside everything to my name if needed, just to have you in my arms as my wife."

Pulling back, he tilted her head up, and he was helpless when he saw passion in her eyes. His mouth sought hers with hunger. Though timid, Elizabeth was quick to learn. His body was on fire, and yet he only desired to hold her closer. His hands gently caressed her face, her arms, her back. Elizabeth's hands wrapped around his waist, then stroked up his chest and settled around his broad shoulders.

Enthralled in their activity, they did not hear the carriage arrive with the Collins party nor the parlour door open. With a gasp, Mrs. Collins ushered Miss Lucas upstairs though her husband remained.

"Cousin Elizabeth! You wanton girl! Unhand Mr. Darcy at once!" Mr. Collins's words crashed on their heads like a bucket of water.

"Mr. Collins, you will never insult my betrothed again!" Mr. Darcy's countenance brooked no opposition; however, Mr. Collins was too stupid to see the promised threat written all over Darcy's face.

"Betrothed? But...but...Miss de Bourgh is your betrothed!"

"I assure you, she is not and never shall be. Miss Elizabeth Bennet is the only woman who shall ever become Mrs. Darcy."

"She has drawn you in with her arts and allurements! I will speak to Lady Catherine at once, and she will remind Elizabeth of her place!"

"Mr. Collins, I told you to never insult her again. I shall know how to carry my point." Mr. Darcy would have continued with explaining his connection to the Archbishop, but Elizabeth laid a hand on his arm, forestalling him. By the time he looked back from Elizabeth, Mr. Collins had fled the parsonage.

"Elizabeth, forgive me for my ungentlemanly display. I had wanted to convince you of a courtship after this, but now you must see...." He trailed off, unsure how to explain that by his actions she was now forced to marry him, against her will. A deep frown marked his sad face.

"To which display do you seek forgiveness?" Elizabeth interrupted his thoughts.

"Both."

Stroking her jaw in mock thought, Elizabeth paused before answering, "I should say not. I quite enjoyed the display."

She then cast him an arch look. "Both of them."

The passionate side of Darcy wanted nothing more than to capture her about the waist and bring her close while kissing her senseless again, but the gentleman settled for a teasing reply. "Well, if I cannot earn forgiveness, do you wish to extract penance?"

"In due time, Mr. Darcy, in due time."

Before Darcy could reply, a maid brought in tea and some pastries, presumably requested by Mrs. Collins, though the maid fled before they could inquire, undoubtedly due to the recent *displays*. Elizabeth began to pour the tea and offered for him to sit, puzzling Darcy by her seemingly indifferent actions at such a time.

"Mr. Darcy, you questioned my sister's affections as she did not give enough outward display of them to appease your observation. How shall a woman act to reassure the man? Shall one seek to accidentally touch him?" As she spoke, she handed him a cup filled with tea, intentionally allowing her fingers to gently graze his. He shivered.

"Oh, dear, I forgot to put the sugar in." She reached for the cup again, and her fingers touched his once more. She stood slightly to accomplish her task, allowing her napkin to fall. Returning his now sweetened tea to his hand, she spoke again. "Or perhaps she should try to put her charms on display more often? How clumsy of me! I dropped my napkin." She then bent low to retrieve it. Darcy groaned.

"Perhaps she should not hesitate to flatter and compliment the man? My father excelled in debate at Cambridge; I should think you did as well. I have found your arguments most *persuasive*." Darcy could take no more. His tea cup, which had not even made it to his mouth as it stood agape in a stupefied manner, was put down with a clang. In an instant, he was next to her on the sofa, wrapping his arms around her again.

After a long, deep kiss, Darcy breathed, "Elizabeth, you are too generous to trifle with me. If your feelings are still what they were, tell me so at once. My affections and wishes are unchanged, but though we must still marry, one word from you will silence me on this subject forever."

Elizabeth leaned forward for another kiss, but Darcy insisted on knowing her answer. Sighing, she replied, "My feelings are much altered. I see now you are the best man of my acquaintance, and my *feelings* are quite overwhelmed."

Darcy cupped her face, but just before kissing her lips, he turned his head and whispered in her ear. "In that case, allow me to tell you how I have envisioned our children. Daughters with their mother's curly hair and expressive eyes, sons full of liveliness." He trailed kisses from her ear down her neck.

Moaning from his ministrations, Elizabeth murmured, "Oh, and how many children do you envision for us?"

"At least six, my dear, and I am certain it shall take much practice to become a true proficient, as my aunt would say."

Elizabeth playfully replied, "Now, sir, about your penance...."

To be continued...

Rose Fairbanks

An Unladylike Display

Readers enjoyed "An Ungentlemanly Manner" so much they requested a sequel. It's been years, but I finally wrote it!

Elizabeth sat at the vanity in her bedchamber in Darcy House. Three weeks had passed since Mr. Darcy's proposal, her refusal, his rebuttal, and them being found in a compromising manner. And for two weeks they had been under very watchful eyes. They had been discovered by the Collinses in an ardent embrace. After very little talk, Elizabeth found herself in Darcy's arms again, this time entirely of her own coaxing.

Lady Catherine was so disgusted with the news Mr. Collins brought her that she ordered Elizabeth to leave, and all of Darcy's wealth and prestige could not make up for the impression left upon her mind of her daughter suffering from Mr. Darcy's animal appetites. Elizabeth had expected a fight from her ladyship, but instead she seemed to think the couple deserved each other. She muttered about Darcy's untitled lineage being the fault and asserted that she would find another husband for her daughter.

Darcy and Elizabeth left Rosings the next morning and found very little sympathy with her aunt and uncle in London. Darcy met with his solicitor and began arrangements for a special licence, convinced that would ease his way with the Bennets. After tarrying in London for two days, they continued to Longbourn. Mr. Bingley accompanied them.

Elizabeth expected her father to be upset and disappointed at the news of the reason for their marriage, but he was soon brought to reason by Elizabeth explaining that she did esteem and like Mr. Darcy. While they were found in a moment of passion, her changed feelings did not rest entirely on Darcy's physical persuasions.

Once at Netherfield, Darcy called daily. He frequently came with Bingley before breakfast and stayed until after supper. There were times when his patience wore thin with her mother and the frequent visits of her aunt Phillips, but on the whole, Darcy was a devoted lover. She soon understood that she had been quite mistaken with his character.

A week after their arrival in Hertfordshire, Darcy spoke quietly to her in the drawing room. "Elizabeth, we have already talked about my ill-thought words during my proposal, but I truly owe you an apology. Your family is a bit more eccentric and boisterous than I am used to, but they are loving. I was too full of prejudice to see their value. You accused me of pride, and for the last week I have been too happy with our joy to take the time to evaluate your criticisms."

"Do not repeat what I said to you that night!" she cried.

"What did you say that I did not deserve?"

"I was very unfeeling. I had no notion that you had any feelings at all, and now I have seen a man who is more generous and forgiving than I could imagine."

He discreetly grasped her hand and held it between both of his. "My dearest, Elizabeth. I was taught correct principles but left to follow them in conceit. You taught me a valuable lesson."

Again, she had tried to claim that she was not due such charitable thoughts, but he would not hear of it.

Elizabeth smiled again at the memory. He truly respected her opinion and thoughts, such as when he asked her opinion on a matter of business. A few days later, he returned to London to retrieve his sister and her companion. It gave Elizabeth great joy to see him as a brother. He was always very gentle with Georgiana, and she praised him without guile.

The day before their wedding, Darcy pulled Elizabeth aside as she walked him to the door. Bingley and Jane stayed behind for a moment, and nobody seemed interested in chaperoning a couple that was as good as married. Elizabeth hoped Darcy would give her another ungentlemanly display. When he pulled her into his arms, she was not disappointed.

Her confusion was great then, when with her head tilted up and her eyes shut, she did not feel his lips on her. He stroked her cheek but rested his forehead against hers. "You do tempt me to forsake reason, love, but we are very near your family, and I need to discuss something with you."

She pouted for a moment before inquiring, "What can concern you tonight?"

"Bingley has asked your sister to marry him, and she has said yes."

"Oh! I am so happy for Jane! But why has nothing been said, and what are you worried about?"

"They insist on not speaking with your father for several more weeks. They wish for us to have all the attention tomorrow and believe the community would not titter over our marriage as much should their engagement be announced."

"What do I care for that? Jane's happiness is my own!"

"I did tell Bingley that, and he says he discussed it with Jane, but she would not give way. He lingers in the drawing room so we might discuss it."

"She can be so stubborn!"

Darcy laughed. "Is this a trait for all Bennet women?"

"Yes, we learned it upon our mother's knee."

Darcy raised his eyebrows but said nothing, and Elizabeth gave a mock glare. "Do not say it, Fitzwilliam."

"I would not dream of saying you are like your mother, my dear."

She scowled. "That is what my father calls my mother when he is either laughing at her or annoyed with her."

"Oh? I had not noticed." The twinkle in his eye belied his tease.

"I shall exact revenge on you soon. For now, let us go announce the betrothal of my sister and your future brother."

"Good. I rather like your demands for penance," he said before a swift kiss to her lips. He had no compassion on her and left her stunned in the hall while he walked on to the drawing room.

Shaking her head, she quickly followed. She walked to the sideboard and began filling glasses of wine and sherry, then passed them around. The room quieted due to her peculiar activities.

Seeing the expectant looks of her family, she cleared her throat. "It is quite irregular for a lady to offer a toast, but then Mama always reminds me of how I vex her nerves."

Mrs. Bennet blushed, then looked at Darcy and stammered, "She is a very good girl, most of the time. It is only sometimes and to such things as could concern a mother—"

Elizabeth interrupted her. "Shall you hear my toast, Mother? I promise it shall delight you."

Mrs. Bennet silenced, and Elizabeth spoke again. "It is my great honour and brings me much joy to announce the betrothal of Mr. Charles Bingley to Miss Jane Bennet!"

A roar erupted in the room, and the ladies ran to Jane's side. Elizabeth hugged her closely. "You should not have delayed on my account!"

"Thank you, Lizzy! You are my very dearest friend and sister. How shall I get along without you?"

"I think you love Mr. Bingley so much that you will hardly notice I am not there."

"Do not tease! You know I could never replace you. I only hope that one day you will find as much happiness with Mr. Darcy."

The others pulled Jane from her side, leaving Elizabeth with a growing realisation that throughout her engagement to Mr. Darcy, she never once thought of it with anything less than contentment. Surely one should feel at least nervousness if not marrying for love? She had no further time for thought as Darcy walked towards her. "Might we talk again for just a brief moment?"

Elizabeth readily agreed. She was hoping he would now kiss her again, uncertain as she was how to convey her desire for such a thing. Instead of pulling her close, he did not touch her at all, nor would he meet her eye.

"Fitzwilliam, are you unhappy with their engagement? I thought you approved now—"

He quickly interrupted her. "I am very happy for them! I have realised again my selfishness. How did I think I knew Jane's heart? Or what was best for

Bingley?" He paused a moment and spoke very softly. "How did I force you to marry me?"

"You did not force me. I have consented."

"After a forceful persuasion!" He looked up at her, and she saw the pain and misery in his eyes. "Tell me," he said as he reached for her hand, "when I touch you, are you reminded of that day?"

"Yes," she drew out the word, uncertain of his concerns but enjoying his touch.

He let her hand go. "Tomorrow we marry, and I need you to know that I will not force my attentions on you. I will never again take what you are unwilling to bestow."

She had an idea he meant the marriage bed. "We will be married. It will be your right. I knew my duties when I agreed to the marriage."

He shook his head and looked at his feet again. "You refused me because you did not like me. I was selfish, and I realise I awakened some carnal susceptibility on your side, but it is not the same as if you were coming to a husband as you had once wished. You would not come out of love—"

The door to the drawing room opened, and the others filed out. It was time for Bingley and Darcy to leave, and further conversation was impossible. As Darcy boarded his carriage, Elizabeth felt her heart fly from her chest and go with him.

How did a woman tell a man she so hurtfully rejected only weeks before that she now loved him? She lay awake all night considering the best words and how she might say them, but they had no privacy during the wedding breakfast. Once in the carriage together, she was at first too nervous and then fell asleep. Waking upon their arrival in London, she was taken to her new chambers immediately and readied for dinner. Again feeling it impossible to speak the words of her heart, she said very little at all and pushed her food around. Darcy soon suggested they retire for the evening, and he had left her at her door with only a kiss to her hand an hour earlier. It was plain that he was not coming to her tonight.

He did not ask if she had a change of feeling. Nor did he give her any opening. Elizabeth chastised herself for being so upset. Of course, he would not wish to risk rejection again; no man would. Her only route was an unladylike one.

Coming to a decision, she put on her dressing gown. With a candle in hand, she carefully went down the private stairs to a room just outside Darcy's chamber. The home was remodeled during his parents' life and the current floor plan was all the fashion then, although she had read that the famed Robert Adams bemoaned the English preference for husband and wife chambers on separate floors for Town. Of course, he meant for decorating an opulent suite, but Elizabeth thought it rather ridiculous to do all this walking in the middle of the night. Or at least for a lady to do so. She was in danger of tripping over her skirts!

Reaching Darcy's door, she knocked and received no answer. She knocked again, louder, and still heard nothing. Swallowing her pride and in hopes of an invitation into his room, she boldly turned the handle. She would speak her mind and be done with it. She found a room that seemed to see little use. It was clean but looked more like a guest room than one her husband slept in. She looked around. There were no books. Her own room had several of her favourites as well as others not to her taste and some she had not read.

But where was her husband? It was clear that he seldom slept in this room, and he was not there now. She *had* heard about men who took rooms at their clubs...but on their wedding night? Even if he meant not to consummate the marriage, how would it look to his peers? He would never want something so private to be so publicly known about him. That brought to mind other *private* reasons for a man to spend a night out of his home. Her heart constricted.

She did not wish to think it. He loved her and would not disrespect her so. A small voice in her head said that he had claimed to love her three weeks ago when he abused her family and station in life, but she pushed it aside. He had apologised profusely for that and many other things she felt required no forgiveness. It was early yet; perhaps he had some kind of meeting to attend and would return later.

Leaving his chamber, she decided to wait in the library for his return. Silently entering the room, she suddenly stopped as she saw Darcy standing before the fire. He leaned one arm against the mantle, and his head rested on it. His other hand held a brandy glass. He wore only his shirtsleeves and breeches. She had never seen him so informal, nor had she ever seen him so distressed.

"Fitzwilliam?" she asked and tentatively took a step forward.

"Elizabeth!" He suddenly raised his head to look at her. His body tensed, and she saw his fist tighten around the glass.

"I am sorry if you wished to be alone. I did not mean to intrude on your privacy," she said, entirely losing her nerve for coming downstairs at all. Her feelings were too raw. A moment ago, she had thought him not home and struggled to not cast mean reasons upon it. Just before that, she had thought he was purposefully ignoring her. Now he looked upon her with surprise, admiration, and something else she had not seen before.

"Could you not sleep?" he asked, and Elizabeth noted that he did not correct her assumption that he wished to be alone.

"I was merely looking for something to read." She moved to a bookcase and inspected a few titles before grabbing one. "This should be sufficient."

"I wish you a good night then," he said.

Elizabeth was walking towards the door, feeling his eyes follow her, when she realised the ridiculousness that a husband and wife should say good night to one another in such a fashion. Especially on their wedding night!

"Might…" She halted for a moment and gathered her courage. "Might I have a kiss good night? You gave me one before, but as I did not go to bed, I rather think I deserve another one."

"As you wish," he said and walked towards her but without a smile on his face. Bringing her hands to his lips, he gently kissed each one. "I hope you have pleasant dreams, Elizabeth."

Elizabeth licked her lips. "That is a kiss goodbye from a suitor. Does not a wife get a different sort of kiss good night from her husband?"

He raised an eyebrow. "You are questioning my husbandly behaviour already?"

"I am only testing to see if you have truly amended your manners."

"Far be it from me to displease Mrs. Darcy," he said and stepped closer. She watched as his chest heaved up and down, and she felt her own heart race. He gently held her chin between his thumb and forefinger and tipped her face up. She saw his blue eyes search hers before hers fluttered shut. At last he gently kissed her lips, and his fingers trailed down her throat, settling at the base of her neck. Stepping forward, she licked the seam of his lips, desperate for the kind of kisses he gave her weeks before. He wrenched himself away.

"Elizabeth! Have mercy on me, please! If only you knew how difficult this was for me, I know you would never wish to be cruel. You know my affections and wishes, and I have desired to give you time to adjust to being my wife first."

"You stupid man!" she cried as she flung her arms around him. "Do not you know my feelings have altered? I love you!" He tried to speak again. "No, now I will silence you!" She kissed him, and at last his arms wrapped around her.

The next morning as she rushed to dress lest they be late for breakfast, she swatted Darcy away as he attempted to kiss her neck. "Shoo! I have to tie up the collar."

"Oh, Lizzy. I hate seeing you all covered up."

"This is what ladies wear in the morning when there are no visitors. Surely you have seen Georgiana wear something similar."

"I never understood why it is that at home a woman should be covered from head to toe—no, *no,* not the cap," he plucked it from her hands, "but if there are visitors or she is out of the house, she ought to wear short sleeves and a lower-cut dress."

"Neither do I, but I do not make the rules. I would hate for the servants to think me unladylike, though."

He lowered his head and whispered in her ear, "I rather like your unladylike displays."

Elizabeth blushed. "Well, perhaps you might be a *visitor* this evening, and I shall wear the proper attire for your call."

"A visitor? No, I do not plan to return to my room, regardless of the fact that it is where we spent last night."

"I did notice it seemed mostly unoccupied. I think I left my cross on the little table." Elizabeth watched as he found the table without direction. "You seem to know your way around my chamber quite well."

"I have slept in here since November, actually. At first I could not understand why I found no sleep in my bed chamber and thought perhaps there was a draft. I tried other chambers as well and still could not rest. At last I tried this one and slept perfectly. I never took much time to consider the décor, but one day Georgiana asked if my mother had liked long walks as the décor of the mistress's chamber suggested so. That was when I realised the chamber reminded me of you. A few weeks later, I journeyed to Rosings and found you there."

"So you admired me for being a great walker? I shall never forget the looks of horror on Miss Bingley's and Mrs. Hurst's faces when I arrived at Netherfield on foot with petticoats covered in mud. They thought me a hoyden, I am sure."

She stood before him, and he smiled. "I told you, I rather liked your unladylike displays." He untied her collar. "There, just impertinent enough."

Darcy continued to insist that Elizabeth not hide her beautiful neck when at home. Three weeks later, she received an unexpected call from Darcy's aunt, the countess. Charmed by Elizabeth's attire, she soon adopted it and began a fashion trend, giving Mrs. Darcy all the credit. Some declared it unladylike; others quite enjoyed what was displayed.

The End

Teddy

This story was written for my son's third birthday. He's turning five this year! They grow far too fast!

November 11, 1820

Pemberley

Elizabeth looked up from the book she had been reading and sighed. He had been so determined to stay awake until Fitzwilliam returned, but since he was eschewing naps, he was exhausted by seven. *He has grown so much.* In the last year, he had lost most remnants of babyness and looked much more like his older Bingley cousins.

Her heart lurched as she gazed lovingly at the sweet face resting on the pillow. How many times had she prayed for this blessing? How many times had she feared this day would never come?

Elizabeth had been content to enjoy her first several months as a newlywed. She and Fitzwilliam were growing in love, and she was adapting to her role as mistress of the vast estate, Pemberley. Her mother had begun to berate her for failure to fall with child before their six-month anniversary, but it never bothered Elizabeth. Jane produced a son shortly after their first anniversary, and Elizabeth's heart had felt only joy. When another year passed, and another nephew came, she began to grow impatient.

Fitzwilliam claimed he was content, and she believed him, truly she did. Facing the opinions of the rest of society was another matter. Encounters with Mrs. Parke, the former Miss Bingley, who had already performed her duty in producing an heir, were never pleasant. Lady Catherine attempted to prove herself useful with endless advice over Elizabeth's "predicament." Georgiana made her debut later in the Season, and even with the assistance of her aunt by marriage, Lady Matlock, the experience left Elizabeth exhausted and frazzled. Bemused, she began to realise why her husband disliked balls so much.

By the third year, even Elizabeth had to admit that it was difficult to see Jane with child again and Mrs. Parke expecting "the spare." Lydia had borne a son, and even Kitty, lately married, suspected that she was with child. Elizabeth was not made for ill humour and determined not to grow despondent, but nonetheless, she felt empty.

She and Fitzwilliam had so much love to give. Fitzwilliam was made to be a father; he had already done so well with Georgiana. They spoke with physicians and midwives, and they all said the same thing. Nothing irked Elizabeth more than being told not to fret, and then she would easily conceive. For a time, she found herself fretting over if she was fretting too much.

The winter after their fourth year of marriage, her husband's cousin chaperoned Georgiana for the Season. Fitzwilliam spoiled her with an extended visit to Cornwall. By the time they left in May, she had many suspicions that her greatest wish was fulfilled.

Happy was the day in June when the heir to Pemberley made its presence undeniably known. Happier still was his safe delivery on November 11, 1817, just shy of his parent's fifth wedding anniversary.

Their son was tall like his father. His looks were very much like him as well, except for the sparkling eyes he inherited from his mother. They named him Theodore; after so long a wait and so many prayers answered, no other name would do. He carried the middle name of Robert, as every Darcy heir had for five generations.

Elizabeth's thoughts were distracted by the cooing of her infant daughter, called Annie after her Darcy grandmother, in the crib across the room. And she suspected another addition in the late summer. Her heart nearly burst with the joy motherhood had brought her.

Teddy, as they called him, was intelligent and bright. His temperament matched his mother's, cheery and friendly, always active and lively. But he loved his papa and hence why she was in the nursery this evening.

Fitzwilliam had visited the Matlock estate to help on some matters and planned to return last evening but was prevented by rain. The sun broke through for a portion of the afternoon to dry the roads, and Elizabeth knew her husband would be home before this night was through, no matter that it began to rain again nearly two hours ago. Fitzwilliam would never miss his son's entire birthday.

She heard soft footsteps in the hall and turned to see the door inch open.

"Lizzy." Her husband quietly walked towards her, quickly embraced her, and gently kissed her lips. "He fell asleep?"

"Aye, he tried so hard, but without napping, it just proved too much."

"I am sorry I missed this day," he said with real regret.

"It is well, love. He knows you love him, and you can enjoy tomorrow with him. Let's come to bed; you must be exhausted. Has Mrs. Reynolds called for a bath?"

"Hmmm," he murmured. Then he bent down and gently kissed his son's forehead. "I love you son, our gift of God."

The End

Rose Fairbanks

Presenting Miss Darcy

I wrote this for my daughter's first birthday. She is called Annie after her paternal grandmother, so it seemed fitting to imagine her as a Darcy child.

May 30, 1842

Pemberley, Derbyshire

A hush fell over the drawing room as the couple entered. Elizabeth Darcy's conversation ceased as she glanced across the room and made eye contact with her husband. He gave her a soft smile, but it did not reach his eyes, which clearly belied his sadness to her.

As the room watched, mother and father of the bride walked across the room to the newlyweds. Fitzwilliam Darcy took his eldest daughter's hand, not the one with the ring on it that symbolised she was now under another's care, and raised it to his lips. Finally, his daughter's eyes were drawn away from her spouse's and met his own. She gave him a full, radiant smile. *Elizabeth's smile.* It offered him a modicum of cheer.

Having gained the notice of the lovers, Darcy turned to face the crowd and make his announcement. "May I present…" In the short pause, three and twenty years of memories flashed. "Mr. and Mrs. Edward Moore."

Applause rang through the room. Elizabeth placed her arm on Darcy's, and they began to lead the assembled crowd to the dining-parlour for the wedding breakfast. Darcy said little during the breakfast, and on the occasions he met Elizabeth's eyes from across the table, he smiled a little at the memories he knew they shared of their daughter.

*****

May 26, 1820

Elizabeth's labour with her second child was very short but intense. She had been ill much of the pregnancy. She was never very weak, but she had frequent bouts of fever, nausea, and back pain. The midwife assured the nervous parents that all was well, that Elizabeth's complaints were not unusual at all, but it did little to ease the anxiety they felt but did not verbalise. Perhaps it was because she was the second child herself that Elizabeth worried excessively over the transition from one child to two. Between her illness, the usual pains, and her nerves, Elizabeth slept little of the pregnancy and had never been so thankful for Pemberley's library than during those months.

The pains felt differently than they had with her firstborn, Teddy. At first she was certain it was just the onset of her illness again, but before too many hours, it was clear that she was in labour—and something was not quite right.

Neither Darcy nor Elizabeth could truly remember much of that day, only that it ended in joy. Elizabeth's maid had alerted the housekeeper when the pains began, and eventually Darcy was retrieved from his estate affairs. While they awaited the midwife, Elizabeth's illness attacked. In an instant, she was shivering with a high fever, and her belly was cramping acutely. Darcy refused to leave his ill wife and acknowledged that he had never prayed so fervently in his life. When the midwife finally arrived, Elizabeth could only register the look of terror in her eyes as the entire room was silent with a palpable sense of fear and dread. As usual, her courage rose to the occasion, and she chose to chatter as much as possible and attempt to put the room at ease.

Very few minutes later, the midwife passed a beautiful baby girl to Darcy and assessed her patient, who was recovering from the fever exceptionally fast now that the baby had arrived. Her full recovery would take several more weeks, but she was undoubtedly out of danger.

A happy hush descended on the room as everyone looked to the parents. After meeting Elizabeth's eyes and sharing a soft smile, Darcy happily declared, "Allow me to present Miss Anne Frances Darcy."

Even the servants who had never met Lady Anne Darcy could not contain their tears of joy. Pemberley had a new Miss Darcy, and she was named after the beautiful and gentle former mistress.

*****

May 1838

The years passed, and Darcy and Elizabeth were blessed with four more children, an even number of boys and girls. From the moment of her birth, Anne enjoyed being read to. Elizabeth joked that it was due to all the reading she did during the pregnancy. Once Anne was able to read, she had an insatiable curiosity. She was the apple of her father's eye, preferring him to all others since just after her weaning. Her first word was "Papa," and her first steps were to him.

Elizabeth heartily teased Darcy for being wrapped around the finger of his "first baby girl," but he could not repine a moment of it. In truth, all the daughters were doted on by their father, and in turn, the sons were never too old to display their love for their mother. But Anne Darcy was now a young lady of eighteen, busying for her court presentation, and suddenly found great use in her mother.

Miss Darcy was strikingly beautiful and looked very much like her namesake. She had the Fitzwilliam family blue eyes and Lady Anne's fair hair and colouring. Her eyelashes were long like her father's but full and dark, illuminating her fine eyes, like her mother's. The dimples to her smile came from her father, but the expression she had, the smile that could light the room, came from her mother.

Her temperament was a mixture of her parents as well. Mostly, she was quiet and gentle like her grandmother Darcy, but she had a mischievous streak like her mother and was obstinate like her father. She was accomplished, well read, and genuinely intelligent, with a clever but sweet wit. Between her beauty and her disposition, she had many suitors her first Season out but was determined to marry only for a deep love.

Darcy took the Season particularly hard. At her coming out ball, he danced the first set with her and could only think of the first time he danced with her in his arms. She was only weeks old when he found Elizabeth dancing around the ballroom of Pemberley with her. The sight was so charming, he happily pulled his wife and daughter into a form of waltz embrace. As Anne aged, so did the dancing. In the blink of an eye, she went from being carried in his arms to stepping on his toes to learn the steps to being praised by her dancing master.

Now, Darcy and Elizabeth watched as their eldest daughter took up her position in line to enter the throne room and make her curtsy before Queen

Adelaide. They beamed with pride to hear announced: "Presenting Miss Anne Darcy of Pemberley in Derbyshire."

*****

May 1841

The Darcys held a combined ball for their eldest son's graduation from Cambridge and Anne's one and twentieth birthday. The house was overflowing with young people, many of them Teddy's friends from school.

Darcy and Elizabeth had their eye on one gentleman in particular, though. His eyes followed their daughter around the room, and now he was in conference with their son. Neither could say what it was about this gentleman that garnered their attention, although it might have been how Anne surreptitiously looked about the room for him when she believed no one was watching. Darcy and Elizabeth conveniently found themselves near enough to their son and daughter to hear the introduction when it was finally made.

"Eddie, may I present my sister, Miss Darcy of Pemberley? Annie, this is my good friend, Mr. Edward Moore of Spotborough."

The young couple stood still for some time before they made the appropriate bow and curtsy. Mr. Moore clearly seemed dumbstruck by Anne, but she had never known such an affliction in her life.

"Thank you for the introduction, Teddy, but Mr. Moore and I are already acquainted."

"You are?" Teddy was clearly quite surprised.

Anne smirked. "Of a sort." She raised an eyebrow in challenge at Mr. Moore.

Teddy gave his friend an expectant look, and Moore closed his eyes in resignation.

"Miss Darcy is only partially correct. We were never introduced. I had been roped into taking my sister shopping, and after several *excruciating* hours in various shops, I was in a foul mood. Lucy was modeling a new hat in a milliner's shop and was insistent on some specification as to why I liked it. Instead of focusing on what I liked about that hat, I foolishly, and loudly, criticised certain features on other hats."

Teddy rapidly nodded, and his parents shared a knowing look. They could all quite predict what happened next and heard a short huff come from Anne.

"Lucy happily skipped off, and suddenly Miss Darcy was in view with a hat quite like what I criticised."

"Tell him exactly what you said, Mr. Moore. Teddy, I want you to know the true character of the sorts of men you call friends!"

Sighing in resignation, Mr. Moore accepted his chastisement. "I said hats with flowers on them were only tolerable and not handsome enough for a scullery maid, let alone my sister; feathers were much better."

Before Teddy could say a thing, Anne spoke again. "Well, Mr. Moore, you are in *my* home. I believe you have heard of Pemberley before? And my father, certainly?" Moore nodded. "And do I look like a scullery maid to you tonight? Are the Fitzwilliam jewels I wear insufficient because I have not decorated my hair with ridiculous plumage?"

Moore gulped, and Teddy tensed, but Darcy and Elizabeth could only barely keep themselves from laughing. Moore looked down to his feet for a moment and then met Anne's eyes.

"No, madam, you are easily the handsomest lady in this room." She blushed and gasped, but he continued. "Pray, forgive me. As I said, I was in a foul mood, and I only said what I knew Lucy desired to hear so she might leave me alone. Your hat was lovely, but I do think it was due more to the lady wearing it than the construction."

Anne held his eye for a long moment before smiling brightly at him. Of the observers of their interaction, only she was oblivious to the effect it had on him. Standing a little taller than he had before, Mr. Moore came to his point at last. "Miss Darcy, might I have the pleasure of your next available set?"

Anne seemed to accept with true gladness and was soon led to the floor. Straining their ears, Darcy and Elizabeth heard Moore ask their daughter, "What think you of books?"

Moore was easily a handsome man, but upon hearing Anne's laughter, his smile stole the breath of nearly every lady in the room. "Oh, Mr. Moore! I can never speak of books in a ballroom!"

At that moment, Darcy and Elizabeth knew their daughter was lost to them and would not long bear the name Darcy.

*****

May 30, 1842

The formal wedding breakfast was over, and many of the guests had departed. It was well past time for Anne and her husband to leave, but she clearly lingered.

Anne had said goodbye to her parents but still seemed to look around the house as though she could not bear to leave, when her eye was caught by a nursemaid descending the steps with a baby in her arms.

As only family remained, the nurse handed the baby to Anne's sister-in-law. Teddy had married nearly a year ago and had very recently been blessed with a baby girl. Teddy managed the family estate in

Lincolnshire, and the little family had only arrived that morning.

Anne tugged on her husband's arm and said, "Come, love. I have an introduction to make."

Taking the precious bundle from her sister-in-law's arms, she looked to her husband for a moment. "May I present Miss Darcy?"

Anne Moore's smile outshined all others she gave before as she met her parents' eyes and soon passed the baby back. After one final kiss and hug to her family, she left her childhood home on the arm of her husband, and although she did not see it, her mother's and father's smiles finally met their eyes for the first time all day. Pemberley was presented with a new Miss Darcy.

The End

The Forget Me Not State

In the autumn of 2013, I participated in a short story challenge from a list of "wacky holidays." One suggestion was "marooned without a compass." I had this story in my head partially based on similar experiences I had traveling in Alaska and Canada, but I couldn't figure out how to end it, and it just sat for over a year until finally inspiration struck again.

Somewhere on the Alaska·Canada Highway

"Beautiful Lizzy. So beautiful. Don't forget me…if only…" The handsome man in Elizabeth's dreams murmured in her ears and gave feather·light kisses to her eyelids, cheeks, and nose.

She turned into them, seeking his mouth, and let out a moan, but suddenly he was not there. Her consciousness sharpened when she heard a throat clear. She opened her eyes to see Will Darcy sitting at the nearby banquette of her fifth wheel and looking at her with an expression she could not make out.

First meeting three months ago, the duration of their acquaintance did not improve their relationship. He was rude and condescending the first night they met and nothing had changed since. If Elizabeth didn't love her sister, Jane, so much she would be angry that she had invited her new boyfriend, Charlie, on their annual trip. Especially as it seemed where Charlie went so went his sister, Caroline, and best friend—the annoying Will.

"Good morning, Elizabeth. Are you feeling better?" he asked with what appeared to be genuine concern.

Sheepishly, Elizabeth began to rise. She was sure her face was covered in drool and her hair a disheveled mess. She had some odd reaction to some weeds she walked through the day before when they stopped at Kluane Lake, her favorite place in the world. Benadryl always made her sleep hard, but she did feel better.

"Yes, thank you."

She looked around the room and noticed that Caroline was not present. Elizabeth soon heard her shrieking, "Lost! Charles, what can you mean, we are lost? It is not as though we are in a metropolitan area where there are also moose and buffalo crossing signs!"

"I...I was distracted." Elizabeth barely heard Charles Bingley's reply but imagined his distraction was due to her angelic sister Jane.

There was nothing to be done for; she was going to have to go out there and take the situation by the horns. She made for the door to the fifth wheel and collided with Will.

Elizabeth huffed, and he allowed her to leave first. Outside, Jane met her with apologetic eyes.

"I'm sorry, Lizzy. I know you trusted me while you slept, but I must have dozed for a bit, and when I awoke, I had no idea where we were. I hadn't thought we were lost until Charles mentioned he was unsure, and then I realized the last few townships seemed unfamiliar. We tried guessing on the map, but you know..."

Elizabeth tried not to sound too disappointed or angry. "Jane, we have travelled the Al-Can every year for our sisterly trips for four years now. How could you get us lost?" She looked first to Jane and then to Charles. The yearly fifteen-hundred-mile journey from Fairbanks, Alaska, to Dawson Creek, British Columbia, was very straightforward.

"I...um...was distracted," they replied simultaneously.

Elizabeth looked toward Will, and they both rolled their eyes. Elizabeth loved Jane and thought Charles seemed nice, but acting like stupid teenagers was ridiculous. And the last thing Jane needed after last time. Her sweet sister had survived a fairy tale romance turned abusive relationship.

Caroline looked at her phone and began to wail. "I have no service. We have no service, no 4G or even 3G. We're doomed!"

"Uh, yeah, Carrie, moose don't really need 3G service," Elizabeth cut into her theatrics.

Caroline caught sight of Will with her barracuda eyes. "Will, darling, I just knoooow you will sort this out."

"Actually, Elizabeth has the best chance since she's familiar with the Al-

Can." Elizabeth thought she almost heard a compliment from the hateful man.

Caroline let out a huff. "Maybe. But you're the Eagle Scout and the hunter and used to taking command with your job as a…" Caroline trailed off. She could never pay attention long enough to the miniscule details like Will's job, just the salary figure.

"I'm a…" Will was cut off by Caroline again.

"OMG, what if we're stuck out here, and a bear attacks us! Or-or-or a psycho killer comes! We're all alone in literally the middle of nowhere." The girl genuinely seemed panicked.

"We're going to be fine. Charlie, how much gas do we have?" Elizabeth intervened.

"We're almost on E; that's why I stopped." Elizabeth's eyes grew wide, suddenly understanding the situation was a bit more serious than they first thought.

"So let's use those can thingies and go," Caroline said.

"Um, I used them already."

"Any idea how long it's been since there ws a stop?" Elizabeth asked.

"It's been at least forty miles."

Jane chimed in, "Well, that isn't so bad since there is usually something every sixty miles or so. We can check the Milepost."

Elizabeth somewhat testily explained, "That does us no good when we aren't sure if we're still on the Al-Can or on another road."

Surely they must be on another highway, for they should be within a few hundred miles of Dawson Creek, and there were settlements about every twenty miles on that leg of the road.

"Oh," Jane and Charles responded in kind, staring at their feet.

"What does that mean?" Caroline's voice was very high.

"It means…" Will's voice was loud and angry, but Elizabeth broke in. It would do no good to alarm the others, especially Caroline.

"It means," Elizabeth glared at Will to silence him, "we need to decide between waiting here for someone to happen by or walking and hoping for a house or, if we're lucky, a town."

"I can't walk for miles and miles!" Caroline screeched. Elizabeth wondered what all the Pilates classes Caroline supposedly missed attending did for her then.

"We'll break up into two groups. Charles, you stay with Jane and Caroline. Elizabeth and I can walk in search of a town or house," Will compromised. Begrudgingly, Elizabeth noted the wisdom in it.

Caroline was unconvinced, "Wiiiiilll, you can't leave me here!" She clutched his arm desperately. She apparently had not gotten the memo that she was not his girlfriend—she was about five minutes older than his baby sister —and the poor guy actually had to shake her loose.

"I think I should go with you, Will," Charles suggested.

"Caroline and Jane are not up for what could be a very, very long walk."

Elizabeth acknowledged privately that it was likely more than twenty miles, and it seemed Will understood as well. "Help might come by, and someone should stay with the vehicle anyway. But no one should be alone, and I think it would be best if you stay with the ladies. I'm sure the walk will not even challenge Elizabeth."

Elizabeth narrowed her eyes. Another almost compliment, but it also sounded like he was being chauvinistic in insisting that the ladies needed a man to stay with them. Then again, it would be chauvinistic to insist that none of them could manage the distance. It seemed unlike Will to be so aware of potentially saying the wrong thing or giving offense. Elizabeth finally settled for the fact that Caroline needed to stay put, and Will did not want to be the babysitter.

Will and Elizabeth each took one gasoline can with them. Elizabeth also packed some snacks, water, an extra blanket, and a first aid kit in her backpack, to which her emergency pop up tent was tied. Will carried his own backpack. To the inexperienced, they looked quite prepared for any misadventure. They eyed each other warily, and Elizabeth tried to not think

about the fact that they were walking
unprotected in uninhabited wilderness
where large and dangerous animals
roamed.

If they weren't on the Alaska-Canada
Highway any longer, then who knew when
someone would drive by? Very few tourists
drove on the other highways; it could be
hours or a day or two before someone could
assist them. Walking may also take a day
or two. The camper was well stocked; the
others would be fine. Elizabeth, however,
knew she and Will could have a tough few
days ahead of them.

Knowing there was nothing for forty
miles at least behind them, they pressed
forward. They had walked several miles in
silence when Elizabeth decided they must
speak some. "Not quite the relaxing
vacation to Alaska you imagined, is it
Will?"

He looked at her intently. "I never
imagined it would be relaxing. Meeting new
people, doing new things, constant
activity—that's not relaxing for me."

Elizabeth was surprised. She had
imagined him enjoying a busy and full

lifestyle. "You sound like you were determined to be displeased from the start," she accused.

Will gave a light chuckle. "Perhaps. I do enjoy having the time away from my responsibilities, seeing new places. I just enjoy solitude, the slower things in life. If Bingley wanted to fish all day or hike, I'd be set."

"I'm surprised to hear that you would rather fish than enjoy a night out since you live in Washington D.C. So what was the allure of Alaska for you then?"

"The distance," he mumbled, then caught sight of Elizabeth's curious expression and said louder, "Who could turn down such an opportunity? And I'm from rural Virginia, actually. I only live in D.C. four days a week, working at my uncle's law practice, and then I return to my family farm. If I am fortunate, I can retire very early and devote all my time to managing the estates."

Elizabeth raised her eyebrows. *Estates?* No wonder Caroline hung on him; he sounded loaded. She decided to turn the conversation more to work-a-day things she might understand.

"You're a partner already, aren't you?" He nodded. "And your aunt and some others are in politics, aren't they?"

"Yes..." Will seemed to be growing nervous, although Elizabeth could not fathom why.

Seeing that he was dealing with some personal demon, Elizabeth changed the topic. "Charlie said that you guys drove cross country and then took a ferry to Haines and drove in." She laughed a bit. "That must have been delightful with Caroline. Did you enjoy the drive versus flying?"

Will shook his head. "Caroline did fly, and she met us at Seattle. No way could a man travel across the country with her. Naturally, she was not supposed to come but..." he trailed off. They both knew that Caroline only followed Will. "But I did enjoy the earlier drive. I have always wanted to drive across the country. There's so many things to see. I don't fly commercially, so there are a lot of things I would not see otherwise."

Elizabeth rolled her eyes. Just like the imperious Will Darcy to be too proud to fly commercially. He understood her thoughts. "I think you misunderstood me. I fly a Cessna Skyhawk, but a lot of the larger airports don't allow them to land."

Elizabeth was surprised to hear that he had a pilot's license. She had one, of course; it was quite common in Alaska. "So you won't fly commercially. I suppose you don't trust other pilots? Why not just buy a jet?"

Will laughed. "I have no need for a jet. I seldom have to travel, and when I do, it can be on my terms." He paused a minute and then said coldly, "But yes, I do not trust other pilots."

Elizabeth looked at him in puzzlement. There seemed to be a deeper reason than just arrogance. He sighed, looked ahead and explained, "My parents were killed in a flight when I was eighteen. The pilot made an error and..."

"I understand. You don't have to talk about it," Elizabeth said with gentleness as she touched his arm.

He looked at her gratefully. "So we have established I enjoy flying and driving. I know you fly," he gave her a little grin, "and obviously you enjoy driving if you've driven the Al-Can yearly for four years."

"I do!" She chuckled and then turned serious. "But our trips didn't start out because I enjoyed driving as much as a need for distraction. It was a way to make a fun new memory to cover the bad ones. Each drive is different and unique, as you have seen for yourself."

"Bad memories?"

"Not mine, actually, so it's not for me to share. Suffice to say that I am very protective of Jane and am keeping both eyes on Charles."

Will nodded in understanding. "He's a good guy. He's so easy going that he can be easily taken advantage of. I am glad to see him interested in someone who is genuine and artless. And I know what it is to be protective of a sister."

Hoping to turn the focus away from reasons to protect Jane, Elizabeth seized on the new topic. "Yes, I have heard she is much younger than you. It must have been very difficult for you both after your parents passed." She had kindness in her eyes.

"Yes, it was. I was named her guardian. She was only seven at the time, and now she's seventeen, starting college in the fall. I have been almost a father to her more than a brother, I am afraid. Perhaps if not…" He shook his head and changed topics again. "We should stop and rest for a bit."

Elizabeth agreed and brought out a snack of dried fruit and some water. The walk itself was not very fatiguing, but it was awkward carrying the gasoline cans. Although the cans were light, their hands and arms were cramping. Elizabeth wondered how much more tired they would be on the way back, carrying full cans, but she was also half convinced they would find no settlement and might honestly be stranded for a day or so until another intrepid traveler happened upon them.

After a half hour's rest, they resumed their trek, finding small things to talk about to avoid silences. The sun stayed high until quite late in this area, although not as high as in Alaska. They were exhausted long before sundown.

"How far do you think we have walked?" Elizabeth asked Will.

"I think it must be nearly twenty miles. How are you feeling?" He looked at her with the same look of concern from the morning.

"My feet are sore, but I don't think they're blistered. I truly have no idea where we are. I can only hope we can find something tomorrow." Elizabeth chewed her lip in thought.

"I packed a compass; I know we are heading north, and we should be going southeast, but I am sure you are correct. We will come upon something or someone tomorrow." He hardly seemed to believe his own words.

"Will..." Elizabeth eyed his bag and didn't quite know how to broach the subject.

"Yes?"

"I only brought one tent."

"I didn't bring one at all; Charles assured us we'd be sleeping in the fifth wheel."

"That was the plan, but I brought an emergency tent in case I wanted some solitude."

"Ok."

"It's a *very small* pop up tent, and you are...huge!" Her eyes ran over his frame. He was definitely over six feet tall. And ruggedly handsome at the moment... Was it the outdoors that made him more appealing or that he went a whole day without offending her?

"Oh."

"It's fine. We can be adults about this. I'll put up the tent if you want to start the fire." Although it was summer, the temperature could still drop and be chilly overnight. They got to work and ate a light dinner of snacks they both had brought.

"All right, my sleeping bag is already in there. You got yours?"

"Uh...no, I didn't bring one."

"What happened to 'Be Prepared'? Um...all right, I'll unzip the bag, and I brought an extra blanket. We should be fine with the fire."

Elizabeth was trying not to blush. She was sharing a bed with Will Darcy! The man who had done nothing but look at her in criticism since they met and declared that she was barely cute upon first sight. She could only wonder who might be more mortified.

Arranging themselves in the tent proved even more embarrassing than she ever could have imagined. They only fit by lying on their sides, Will curled up behind her. They were definitely spooning like the most intimate lovers, and she could feel his breath on her neck.

He surprised Elizabeth, though. He did not complain or seem angry. He offered to sleep outside, but it looked like rain, and Elizabeth insisted he sleep inside. He appeared nervous about touching her. It was almost adorable, if she hadn't been so sure he could never be attracted to her and so certain that unlike herself, this was not an unknown situation for him.

Hoping to break the atmosphere—for surely tension could not be the correct word—she asked Will to talk about his hometown and fell asleep quickly, listening to the sound of his voice.

She awoke from the same dream she had since beginning this journey. It was a dream of a handsome man and his love for her evident in his every look, his every touch, his every kiss. He spoke words of endearment...and regret.

She began to rise when she remembered where she was. The location of Will's hands, the proximity of his lips to her ear, and the sudden look of guilt on his face could not hide that he had been the force behind her dream.

They lay in a deafening silence for several minutes. Elizabeth broke it. "What do you mean when you say, 'Don't forget me. If only?'"

Will looked shocked. Undoubtedly, of all the questions she could ask that was not one he was expecting. "If only you did not live four thousand miles away from me! You are everything I've ever wanted in a woman!"

Elizabeth thought she had been shocked enough to find her dreams were brought on by the ministrations of Will Darcy, but to hear this was beyond belief. "You said I wasn't even cute enough to ask for a dance!" Before they were even properly introduced, he had insulted her at the Salmon Bake run by her parents' tourism company.

He cringed. "I'm sorry. I never meant for you to hear. I hate crowds and events like that. Everyone selling something. No one makes a real friendship; they want you to buy something."

Elizabeth smirked just a bit. "Well, it *is* a tourist trap." He laughed lightly. "Would you have ever spoken to me of your..." She wasn't sure at all what he actually felt.

"My love?" Elizabeth gasped. Stroking her cheek, he looked deeply in her eyes. "I love you."

How had this happened? Until three days ago, they barely had a civil conversation. He had shown no signs of admiration in these three months, and yet he loved her?

He must have seen her confusion. "I love you, but how can we ever be together? I can't leave Virginia and D.C., and you love Alaska. We've only known each other a few months."

Elizabeth was silent for a moment as she tried to think through what she wanted, what she felt. He spread one arm underneath her head and pulled her head back down to his shoulder. They were nearly nose to nose, and she could hear his heartbeat. He tenderly stroked her cheek, as though he would never be allowed more and she was the greatest treasure in the world.

Her mouth felt dry, but she needed to tell him. "I'll be attending George Washington for grad school in the fall. I actually went there for a year in undergrad before leaving because of Jane's...situation. My aunt and uncle live only a few miles from your farm. I've even set up to have an internship at a museum a few miles away from there next summer. I've always loved that area; I had hoped to work at one of the living history museums after graduation." Her heart began to beat wildly as Will's face lit up with joy. "If *you* don't forget about me when you get home, I will soon be very close to you."

"I'll never forget a moment spent with you!" Their lips met again and again until they heard a truck approach.

Before they fully calmed themselves, they heard Charles yell out, "Will? Lizzy?"

"It's them! I know that's her tent!" Jane's voice announced her relief.

Elizabeth emerged from the tent first. "Looks like you met with some friendly people! Did you find out where we are?"

Jane replied, "Only a few miles from Fort Liard. We're actually in the Northwest Territories now and about one hundred miles from the Al-Can. Once we get back on the road, we're less than twenty miles to Fort Nelson. Charlie saw the sign for Fort Liard and got it confused with Fort Nelson and thought we were to turn."

"Fort Nelson! That means we may reach Dawson Creek by nightfall!"

Caroline finally emerged from the camper to stand next to her brother just as

Will came out of the tent. Elizabeth was still standing very close to it, and the unruly hair of them both, and Will's misbuttoned shirt said enough to her. She let out a strangling sound and then passed out, caught just in time by Charles.

The remaining four looked at each other for a moment before Elizabeth shrugged her shoulders. "I suppose it's been just too many frightful moments for her on this trip!" Then she added, "Dawson Creek has an airport…"

Three weeks later, Elizabeth and Will were in Haines, Alaska. He was to board the ferry to take him back to Seattle. From there he would pilot several small crafts he arranged to rent back to Virginia. Charles arranged to take a temporary leave of absence from his job until Christmas. He hoped to transfer full time to Alaska by then.

Will held Elizabeth close and kissed her forehead. He whispered in her ear, "I love you. Don't forget me, Lizzy."

She shook her head and fought back tears. "I won't forget you, Will."

Another three weeks saw a nervous but joyful Will greeting Elizabeth at Reagan Airport in Virginia. Elizabeth's aunt and uncle were there as well but allowed Will to greet her first. She ran into his arms and kissed him soundly.

"I didn't forget you, Will. I love you."

The End

Rose Fairbanks

Come What May

For the launch of A Sense of Obligation, I hosted a party on Facebook. I created a question and answer list of wedding day scenarios, and this story is a result of the choices made by the attendees.

Elizabeth Bennet awoke the morning of her wedding day to her mother shrieking. Why had she decided to marry from her home? Her mother took great pride in the gardens, and they were beautiful, but if they had married from anywhere else, Elizabeth may have won the battle about staying in her own apartment on her last night as a single woman.

"Mrs. Darcy!" her mother screamed outside the childhood bedroom she had shared with Jane.

Seeing her sister still asleep, Elizabeth tossed a pillow at her head.

"Hey!" Jane said, her pretty blonde hair still in place.

"Up!" Fanny Bennet said as she stormed in the room. "It will take hours and hours to get you ready! You have an appointment with the hairdresser in seventy minutes! Lord knows if you're not perfect he will probably leave you right there at the altar, and then think of what the neighbors will say! And the cost! How can you be so selfish, Lizzy? Get up now!"

"Mom, William would never do that. He loves Lizzy."

Their mother had already left the room, but Elizabeth gave Jane a hug. "Are you sure you're ok with seeing Charles again?"

"Of course, I am."

Elizabeth chewed her bottom lip. She was less certain that her sister's fragile heart had wholly mended after the terrible breakup with her on-again-off-again boyfriend of the last year. Jane still hadn't told her everything that happened at the rehearsal dinner last week, but just when Elizabeth expected Charles to propose, Jane was saying they had broken up for good. But he was Will's best man, and it was rather late to do anything about it. Sighing, she headed to the shower.

Seventy minutes later, Elizabeth and her four sisters arrived at the salon. After a manicure and pedicure, she sat in the chair for her hair. Being a low maintenance girl, she asked for a simple, sophisticated ponytail with shiny curls. With a sinking feeling, she saw her mother speaking with the manager and shoving a manila folder, undoubtedly full of pictures of more elegant hairstyles, into the woman's hands. Determined to not let all the wedding fuss get to her, she resigned herself to whatever her mother ordered. The woman approached Elizabeth with trepidation.

"Miss Bennet, I'm so sorry but your mother..."

"It's perfectly all right. Really, just as long as it fits under my grandmother's veil, I don't care."

The woman let out a deep breath. "If you're certain..."

"Don't worry about it."

"Ok, then..." she trailed off as the receptionist from the front called her forward. "Please excuse me for just a moment."

Elizabeth popped in the ear buds to her iPod and was content to listen to her favorite mix until the woman returned, again with a look of trepidation.

"It seems that we have double-booked the salon this morning by accident and are understaffed. The other bride's wedding is an hour before yours."

"Oh, it's no problem! My mother planned on everything taking so long. I'm sure we've got plenty of time. We'll just dress first."

"Thank you for being so understanding. If you need anything, please let Kelly up front know."

The manager left, and Elizabeth turned to tell her mother the change of plans. In a matter of minutes, her father arrived with the bridesmaids' dresses, and the ladies took turns popping in and out of the restroom in the back. When Lydia came out first, Elizabeth was confused.

"Lyddie...what are you wearing?"

"The rockin' dress you picked out! Way to go, Lizzy!"

"This isn't what Jane and I agreed on."

"Huh…well, it's awesome. Look at my legs! They're going to look even better in these heels!"

Elizabeth sighed and was silently thankful that her sister was at least over eighteen now. "Jane?" She called to her sister, who was chewing her nails and trying to not look guilty. "What happened?"

"Well, you had to leave the appointment early!"

"I was taking my master's examinations! It was kind of an important thing!"

"It's just that after you left, the attendant said they couldn't have that dress for another six weeks, but they had these, and I didn't know what to do. I couldn't bother you, and you had gone on and on about how you didn't care about things like that. So I texted Carrie and…"

"You let *Caroline Bingley* select the bridesmaids' dresses for my wedding to the man she nearly stalked for years?"

"Come on! You know she never stalked him! She loved him. And you don't know what loving someone who doesn't love you back can do! You don't know!" Jane burst into tears, and Elizabeth's anger died. The dresses were cute. She'd wear them to a party. They would totally steal the show from her understated bridal gown, but what did she care? She got the man, and she had made her sister cry.

Jane took a deep breath and composed herself. "I'm so sorry, Lizzy! I shouldn't be crying on your wedding day!"

"Jane, honey. It's ok. I'm sorry for snapping at you. The dresses are beautiful. Here, you go next for your hair."

Elizabeth was attempting to put mascara on and wondering how women didn't poke their eyes out with the wand when her sister, Kate, began sneezing.

"Kate, you need to stop that sneezing. You'll ruin the wedding," her mother chided.

"I'm not doing it on purpose!" she wailed, and Elizabeth saw that her eyes were puffy and red rimmed as well.

"Are you ok, Kate?"

"I was fine until the bouquets were brought in."

"What do you mean? Why were they brought here?"

"We have to get ready for everything here!" her mother replied. "Now, Will's sister and aunts should be arriving any minute now. The photographer is here already so we can take pictures of all the primping!"

Elizabeth began to wonder how many wedding planning movies her mother had watched during her engagement. She was relishing this entire ordeal far too much. Kate began scratching at her arms. Elizabeth's eyes went wide.

"Kate, I think you're allergic to something."

"Your grandma Glenda was allergic to some flowers like that."

This is not happening, Elizabeth thought. "Do you know which kind?"

"Chrysanthemums, mostly."

"Chrysanthemums!" Elizabeth gasped. "I picked that kind because you said they were Grandma Glenda's favorite."

"Why would I say that? She never cared for flowers much."

"I asked if there were any flowers she was particularly fond of or not fond of and..." she trailed off. She had been so scatter-brained while planning this wedding, studying for her finals, and worrying about defending her thesis. Her mother would have answered chrysanthemums to that question, and Elizabeth would have understood only what she wished.

Mary, who had overheard the concern, came forward. "Well, we just won't have bouquets then. I think this entire wedding thing is far too gaudy."

"No bouquets!" their mother shouted. "No, we'll think of something! And what did I tell you about that eyeliner today? Take it off!"

Mary glared before scampering off to redo her makeup. She enjoyed pretending she was somewhat "goth" and eschewed all things mainstream, but when it came down to it, Elizabeth thought Mary just liked the attention and wasn't that committed to the philosophy. Their mother corralled the other girls to get the bouquets out of the shop.

Will's sister, adopted aunts, and cousin arrived at just that moment, followed by Elizabeth's aunt, Meg Gardiner. "Oh, Meg!" her mother cried. "We are all in an uproar. Kate has my mother's allergies to chrysanthemums—which Lizzy never would have ordered if she would have let me plan the whole thing, but she was so headstrong—well, never mind. We can't have a speck of them around today, and now there's nothing for the girls to carry!"

"The wedding of William Darcy is the most talked about event this season. It is imperative that it does not appear as some kind of thrown together backyard barbeque!" Will's Aunt Cathy declared. Her daughter, Anne, giggled. "What are you laughing about?"

"I was looking up bouquet alternatives on my phone. Here's one for wine corks. I think us Fitzwilliam ladies might be able to gather up enough."

Cathy blushed. "Hush, Anne. You know the doctor even recommends a glass or two of wine at dinner each night."

"Uh huh," Anne said and bit back a smile.

"Elizabeth," a hairdresser called her name. It was finally her turn. Aunt Meg walked to her.

"Go, we will find an alternative. Nothing will ruin this day. Relax!" The two women hugged, and Elizabeth took a deep breath to calm her nerves.

Upon sitting in the chair, she wished her hairdresser would do the same. The woman was young, exhausted, and clearly frazzled.

"Just like in the picture?" she asked.

"Yep, that's fine."

"Ok then," and the woman set to work.

Elizabeth popped in her ear buds and tried not to notice what seemed like an inordinate amount of pulling and hairspray. When the stylist at last got her attentionso she could look at the finished product, she was speechless. There was something that was supposed to be either a beehive or a victory roll protruding from the side of her head, and she had a braid wrapped around her forehead.

"Mama!"

The woman came dashing over. "Oh, Lizzy! You're so beautiful!" Tears welled in her eyes. Aunt Meg came just behind her with the veil ready to pin in place.

"You truly are lovely, Lizzy."

"Aunt Meg..." She stopped as she looked at her mother again.

"It is just like how I pictured it."

Elizabeth put on a fake smile to please her mother and was thankful she had noted to the photographer that she liked a lot of silhouette poses.

"Lizzy, you've got to move, now." There would have been no time to redo the hair even if she wished it. She was shoved toward the bathroom and shimmied into her proper undergarments and gown. At least this went as she had planned. Almost. First, she fell in love with a short, swingy number, but her mother insisted her gown needed more lace. Then, she adored an all-lace sleeveless gown with a bare back. It was sleek and sexy. Will was certain to love it. Her mother declared that it was too modern. In the end, Lizzy chose a classic A-line white satin gown with a V-neck front and lace sleeves. It wasn't her first choice, but it was perfect.

She piled in the car with Jane and Will's sister, Gina—no limo was rented since she intended to get ready at her home—and was handed a beautiful bouquet made from vintage brooches.

Gina hugged her and then explained, "Anne found the idea online, and Aunt Ellen and Aunt Cathy had someone pick up some of their old ones. These here," she pointed to several stunning pieces, "were my mother's. Several are from your grandmother as well."

Elizabeth blinked back tears. She couldn't think of a more meaningful bouquet to carry, and it would last forever. The car pulled up, and she could see they were the last to arrive. Will's cousin, Richie, greeted them.

"Glad you ladies decided to show up!"

"Very funny, Rich. Is everything set?"

"Yes, but I think if you don't start walking down that aisle, Caroline is going to usurp your place."

Elizabeth frowned. "Someone told Will, right?"

"Yes, he knows. He looks like he's going to pass out, but that's just his usual 'being in front of people' face."

"Well, let's put him out of his misery, shall we? Daddy?" Elizabeth asked while searching for her father. Her mother began shooing everyone into their places, and the groomsmen appeared to seat her and Will's aunts.

"Honey bee, I didn't tell you last night because I didn't want to worry you, but now I hope you can contain your reaction. Pastor Ron called last night. He's in the hospital with food poisoning."

"Oh no! Is he going to be ok?"

"Yes, he's doing much better."

"I'm glad to know it. Since the wedding is still going on, I assume you found a replacement?"

"I did…" he prevaricated, and Elizabeth narrowed her eyes.

"Daddy?"

"He is…well, uh…more impressive than you might guess."

Taking a deep breath, Elizabeth shrugged. "As long as it's legal, I don't care." It was beginning to be her mantra for the whole event.

The bridesmaids had gone down the aisle, and the song she selected for her bridal march began. They walked arm in arm and turned the corner to go down the aisle. The attendees stood, and there was an audible gasp. Elizabeth chuckled. There was nothing else to do about it.

Her eyes met Will's. If he could make out her unique hairstyle, he didn't seem to care at all. And she knew he wouldn't. All he wanted was to marry her and begin their lives. This ceremony was entirely for her own vanity and to please their family. She really ought to know better by now. Her vanity nearly cost her everything with Will. But then, he had been stupid and proud, too.

At last she was in front of her love. He mouthed the words "I love you" to her, and it was only because she was so impatient to be at his side that she paid attention to the minister at all. She listened for the cue for her father to place her hand in Will's and give her a kiss. Suddenly she realized the minister dropped his r's completely. Not in a Boston way, but in a very impressive clergyman way. She and Will tore their eyes from one another at the same time to take in the officiant.

He looked exactly like the pseudo-Medieval minister from the movie *The Princess Bride*. It had to be a joke. Priests didn't still dress like that! Beside her, she felt her father laughing. His breathing was hard, but he didn't let a sound escape. Just when she wanted to step on his toes for playing such a trick on her, she glanced at Will again. He had a small smile on his face, and his eyes shone with amusement. She couldn't help but join in. Her shoulders heaved up and down, and from behind she supposed it looked like she was crying, but she contained her laughter.

At last her father kissed her cheek and took his seat. Will grasped her hands, leaned in, and whispered, "Do you think we could just skip to the end?"

Elizabeth had to bite her cheek to not laugh. From behind Will, she heard Richie cough, but it sounded suspiciously like "Say, man and wife."

She grinned and shook her head. Somehow, they made it through the ceremony without collapsing in laughter. After-ceremony pictures went quickly, but Elizabeth rolled her eyes at the number of times Lydia was called to attention from flirting with a groomsman. Jane and Charlie did their best to avoid one another, but nobody missed the awkwardness between them. Aunt Cathy knew the best poses for everyone, of course.

Finally, they made their way to the reception. They nearly chose a mash up of songs for their first dance but then decided upon "Come What May" as it seemed to capture their route to the altar; everything was worth it. She expected her new husband to be a ball of nerves, but he was nearly as calm as he had ever been.

"You're not nervous?" she asked Will as they were alone on the floor.

"I hope you are not consulting your own feelings with that question. It wouldn't do for a bride to feel nervous with her groom."

Smiling at the tease, she replied, "I'm not even sure that ceremony was legal. Daddy told me the pastor got sick, and he found a replacement, but I can't imagine how he found someone with a costume like that!"

"I've been told that your father called Rich...who knows all kinds of people. I asked no other questions but to confirm that the ceremony was valid. But you have not answered my question."

She laughed. "Today has been long and trying, with surprises at every turn, but the only feelings I have right now are happiness and completeness. Will, when I think of what I almost threw away..."

He silenced her with a gentle kiss; their guests cheered. "You know I bear most of the blame. Today is for new beginnings."

Elizabeth couldn't agree more and returned the kiss. Upon breaking it, her eyes landed on an unexpected person. "Is that why you invited George Wickham?"

"We can't keep them apart, Lizzy. If I kept George from Lydia, it would be no better than when I tried to separate Charles and Jane. We can't decide what is best for others."

"Yes, but she's so young!"

"He stayed away until she turned eighteen"

"She has her whole life ahead of her!"

"She may not want what you want."

"You didn't think that was enough when it was your sister he was trying to feel up."

"I was wrong to let my grudge get in the way if they could have waited until she was older. You taught me true forgiveness. But Gina is happy now."

Elizabeth looked at the young women in question. Gina was talking with guests, something she was surprised to see. When they had first met, she was terribly shy.

She also knew how excited Gina was to begin college in the fall. Lydia declared that she wanted to take a year off and travel with some friends or work before trying to settle down and think about a career. She wondered, too, if some of Lydia's behavior the last few months had more to do with trying to forget her feelings for George.

"I guess you're right. It's their lives..." She trailed off and bit her lip. "Do you know what happened with Charlie and Jane? Jane won't tell me anything."

Will rubbed the back of his neck. "I think maybe I had a hand in that."

"What did you do?"

"Charlie wanted to practice his proposal, and I may have given him a nudge with certain wording. I'm not sure it came out well."

"Will! Why would you try to help there? If you were the last man in the world, I wouldn't ask you for speaking advice."

His grip on her waist tightened a bit. "You've obviously amended some of your other ideas on what you'd do with me as the last man in the world."

She sighed. "You're right. I've never been so happy to be wrong."

He leaned his forehead against hers. "I may need that in writing." She laughed, and he kissed her forehead. "I promise to help Charlie with Jane. If they're meant to work things out, a poor choice of words can't stand between them."

"I suppose you know that from experience."

"I certainly do."

"Hmm...I like the sound of that. I do. The best words I've ever said."

"I was thinking after the speech you could bring Jane to a certain spot, I could get Charlie there, and then they could talk."

"You're going to try and patch this up during the reception?"

"What's the worst that could happen?"

"Ask me that some other day. This dance is the only thing that's gone right!" He raised his eyebrows at her. "Well, and you being here, of course."

She worried that he might be offended, but he just laughed. "I love your fierce loyalty and sense of justice, Lizzy."

The dance ended, and soon they were seated at the head table. Rich leaned over and said that it was time for the speech. Charlie wasn't at his seat, and before they could even look for him in the crowd, Aunt Cathy was taking the microphone from the DJ. Elizabeth held her breath. The woman made no secret of her dislike of all things Elizabeth Bennet, although she had seemed helpful earlier today at the salon.

"Willie was just a teenager when he came to live with me," she said, and Will blushed red. "His mother was always like a sister to me, and I was humbled his parents left Will and Gina in my care. I know there were times in life when I was hard on him. I always expected him to make his parents proud. There have been times when I've disagreed with how he did that, but I always wanted what was best for him. Will, I know your parents would be proud of all you've accomplished and very pleased with Elizabeth because she makes you so happy. Congratulations to you both."

It was as near a blessing on their marriage as they would probably ever get from her, and when put that way, Elizabeth found a great deal of compassion for the woman. They stood in unison and walked to her, hugging her tightly until she pushed back and playfully smacked Will's arm.

Soon dinner was being served, and they returned to their seats. Jane and Charlie appeared hand in hand. Elizabeth immediately pulled Jane to her side. "Tell me everything, now!"

Jane blushed. "I was so silly, Lizzy! He was trying to propose!"

"Of course, he was! But what made you angry?"

"Well, he started off with, 'There comes a time when you realize you're going to have to settle,' and I thought he meant he was settling for me, and I just ran away before he could say anything else!"

"He would never mean that!"

"No, that's what he said when I finally let him talk to me tonight. You don't mind do you?" She held up her hand to show Elizabeth her engagement ring.

"No! I'm thrilled for you!" The sisters hugged. "So what was he trying to say?"

"He said he was explaining that he was beginning to think he was going to have to settle for something less than what he hoped for in life, that he couldn't have it all. Then he met me."

"I knew you would work it out!" Elizabeth was soon called away to greet other guests, but she thought that between marrying her best friend and her sister's engagement, nothing could make today better.

Before she knew it, it was time to cut the cake. Her mother insisted they do the Southern tradition of a cake pull, and the single ladies all gathered around. Lydia pulled a hot air balloon, perfect for her desire to travel. Gina pulled a flower, meaning blossoming love. She blushed before glancing at one of the guests she had been chatting with. Caroline got a star, and Elizabeth found that she truly wished all of

Caroline's dreams would come true…as long as they had nothing to do with Will Darcy. Jane pulled the ring, of course; she would be the next to marry. The other charms were less symbolic, meaning things about happiness, security, and longevity.

The single ladies were already gathered, so the bouquet toss was next. She hoped her friend, Charlotte, would catch it but decided against aiming for her. She tossed it high, and there was a bit of a struggle, Caroline and a classmate of Elizabeth's named TaNeshia knocking each other out of the way for it. Anne had just reached out her hand in response to Caroline falling over when the bouquet landed right in her arms. Elizabeth thought Anne looked mortified, but Aunt Cathy smiled as though there were more to the tradition than just an old wives' tale on who would marry next.

The garter toss had an entirely different feeling to it. Will's eyes never left hers as his hand slipped under her dress and seemed to travel far too high for where she had placed the garter, directly above her knee. His look conveyed the promise that they would be leaving very soon. As he tossed it over his shoulder, Elizabeth was

164

struck with the awkwardness of her husband throwing her garments at other men. Strangely, the only one who seemed interested in it was her father's junior partner, Bill Collins, who she always found rather creepy. He lunged and tripped over Rich's feet. The garter hit Ric in the chest, and he caught it by reflex.

During the obligatory subsequent dance, Will whispered in Elizabeth's ear, "Anne has been in love with Rich forever. I was sworn to secrecy. I hope she doesn't read more into this than he means."

Elizabeth looked at the dancing couple. "I don't know. Rich seems to be enjoying himself. Didn't you say earlier that we have to let others live their lives?"

"I did. Will you choose now to learn of my infinite wisdom?"

"If you're so wise, then why do you keep our honeymoon destination a secret from me?"

"For the surprise, darling."

She would argue more, but she loved it when he called her darling. The next song came on, which was to be the final one, but instead of the DJ's voice, they heard Mary's over the microphone. "We're closing out tonight with what I call 'Ode to Mainstream Mix.'"

Elizabeth groaned as Lydia's favorite dance came on, and she began twerking with George. Elizabeth truly thought she might be nauseous, but then she saw Aunt Cathy attempting it and began to laugh. The entire crowd danced in tandem to other overdone songs, such as the "Macarena" and the "Electric Boogie," before finishing it up with the "Chicken Dance."

Finally, Will was pulling her to the door. His red, convertible Mustang was just outside. Their family surged forward for hugs and kisses; they would be gone for a month. And then it was just the two of them, driving into the night.

"Will you tell me where we're going now?" Lizzy asked while she unpinned her hair and shook it free, letting it whip in the wind.

"No, because it's up to you."

"What?"

"Look in the glove box."

She opened it up and found information for Italy and Hawaii. "Oh, Will! How am I going to choose?"

"Well, I thought we'd do one for our honeymoon and then go away before school starts again for you."

"It seems like too much!"

"Making you happy is never too much." He pulled off the road and into a hotel lot. "But for tonight, we will be staying here, and I plan to make you very, very happy several times."

"Will," she scolded and blushed, but it secretly thrilled her when he talked that way.

He checked them in and led them up to their room. In the elevator, he pulled her close. The kiss started with her hand. He turned it over, kissed her palm, and then lingered on her wrist, making her pulse race. His lips had just met hers when the door opened. Without breaking the kiss, he led them to their room. When his head fell down to her neck while still in the doorway, she pulled away just enough to shut the door.

Elizabeth awoke the next morning to her husband kissing her awake. Raining kisses over her face, he started with her eyelids, which fluttered open to see his beaming smile, and ended with her ear. It was a good thing their flight time was so flexible...

The End

Samples from
Zoe Burton
and
Leenie Brown

Excerpts From *Bits of Ribbon and Lace* by Zoe Burton

An Evening in the Darcy Nursery

Little Margaret Jane Darcy leaned over her mother's shoulder, one hand held to her face with the thumb in her mouth, the other hand held out beseechingly to her Papa. Said Papa, otherwise known as Fitzwilliam Darcy, had just entered the nursery to spend a couple of hours with his wife of ten years, Elizabeth, and their four children. Seeing his youngest child reaching out to him over the back of the settee, he plucked her out of her mother's arms, lifting her high in the air to toss her up and then snatching her back to his chest when she squealed. He proceeded to bury his nose in her neck and blow a raspberry, eliciting a similar squeal matched by a wiggle of her body. He chuckled at her response, hugging her close a moment before leaning down to kiss his wife.

Elizabeth ran her hand down the side of his face. "Have you come to join us, my love?"

"I have. Is there room here beside you for me?"

"Always." She smiled lovingly.

No sooner had Darcy sat himself down than the rest of his children looked up from their play and noticed his presence. A chorus of "Papa!" rang through the room as three small bodies hurled themselves at his lap.

"Children," his deep, commanding voice stopped their headlong rush. "Be gentle; you would not want to hurt Margaret."

"No, Papa, we would not. We are sorry. Are we not?" The oldest, Fitzwilliam Matthew Darcy, known to the family as Matthew, asked his siblings. At eight years old, he took his role as guardian and protector of his sisters and brother quite seriously.

Solemnly, the middle two children, Fitzwilliam Bennet Darcy, age six and Elizabeth Rose Darcy, age four, agreed. Bennet and Rose, as they were known in the family circle, were eager to please their parents and therefore quick to obey any request. This did not mean, of course, that they behaved with perfect decorum at all times. Bennet and Rose took after their mother in personality. They never meant to try their nanny's nerves, nor those of their parents. It just seemed to happen. Mud was meant to be played in, stick horses were made to be raced, and trees designed to be climbed. Surely any reasoning person could see this, they agreed. The fact that they were always together in their misdeeds was at least a small relief to their parents. There was far greater chance of losing one than losing both together.

"Very well, then. Your apology is accepted. Carefully, now, you may one at a time climb up for a hug."

When all three had embraced him and gone back to the game, Darcy wrapped his free arm around his wife. Making sure Margaret was well settled on his shoulder, he leaned down to softly kiss his beloved Elizabeth.

"How was your day, Sweetheart," he asked.

"Very well. Margaret drew a picture today."

"She did? Impressive!" He kissed her little head.

****

I'll Never Leave You

"I'm here now, aren't I?!" Fitzwilliam Darcy, Will to those closest to him, roared at his wife. "What more could you possibly want?"

"Yes, you're here! And what are you doing?" Elizabeth waved her hand in the direction of his laptop, quietly humming on the coffee table in front of him. "Are you paying any attention to me at all? And what about your son, who was so looking forward to Dad doing bath time tonight? What about him? Yes, you came home earlier than usual, but you have had your nose stuck in that computer all evening!"

"I don't have to take this crap." With that, he closed the laptop before picking it up and striding to the door. He grabbed his jacket and car keys. "Don't wait up for me.

"Where are you going?" Elizabeth screamed after him.

"Out," he yelled back.

"Just going to walk away, are you? Fine, leave! I don't want someone here that doesn't want to be here with all his heart! I hope that machine keeps you warm tonight!"

As the door slammed shut, Elizabeth collapsed in tears on the floor. For all her bravado, she was scared to death. Her husband had begun months ago to increase the time he spent at work. He told her at first that he was working on a contract deal with a difficult client, but that was a long time ago. Over the course of their courtship and marriage, he had often dealt with similar situations, but those had been resolved in a matter of weeks, not months. She had begun to fear he was seeing someone on the side.

The couple had met at a party in the home of one of Will's best friends, Charles Bingley. Chuck, as he was called by his friends, immediately fell head over heels in love with Elizabeth's older sister. Will and Elizabeth, on the other hand, took a while to warm up to each other. Will was the first to recognize his feelings. Once he did, he chased the reluctant girl of his dreams until she finally gave in and went out with him. They dated for four months, and in that time Elizabeth came to realize that he was the perfect man for her. When he proposed, she eagerly agreed.

Now here they were, five years and two children later. She was no longer the svelte, sexy thing she used to be. Pregnancy had done terrible things to her body. Try as she might, she could not manage to lose that pot belly it left her with. And her hips! She shuddered to think of those. She adored her four-year-old son Ben and eighteen-month-old daughter Jane, and she couldn't imagine life without them, but the process of getting them was brutal.

Who could blame him if he did turn to someone else, she thought. *Look at me. I'm disgusting!*

Excerpt from *Teatime Tales* by Leenie Brown

Two Days in November

19 November 1811

"Bingley, is that not Miss Bennet?" Darcy chuckled as his friend eagerly looked about to find her.

"Where?"

"There, in the group standing before the milliner's?"

"I say, Darcy! It is indeed Miss Bennet. I think I should know her figure anywhere. She is quite the beauty, is she not?"

Darcy agreed, but furrowed his brows. "Is her beauty all that you find to recommend her?"

Bingley drew his horse to a stop and gave his friend a quizzical look. "Why? Do you perceive she has little else to her credit, for I have found her most agreeable and kind? A more gracious woman I have not met! I should hate to think of her as the others from whom you have saved me." He paused. "You cannot believe she is only after my money?"

"No!" The force of Darcy's response shocked not only Bingley, but Darcy as well. Calming, he continued, "I could not do such a disservice to Miss Bennet. Her manners are too open, too accepting, too honest for me to believe her capable of fortune hunting. But, it matters not what I think of her, Bingley. I wish to know *your* intentions." He gave his friend what he hoped was a reassuring look, one that would hopefully stave off some of the displeasure that was certain to follow his next comments. "Are they honourable or are you merely toying with her affections?"

"How could you ask such a thing?" Bingley sputtered. "I would never toy with the affections of a woman such as Miss Bennet. She is not a lady of the *ton*. I do know that paying particular attention to a lady in the country increases expectations far more quickly than it does in town. I am not without sense."

"I never said you were without sense. But there are times when your feet lead and your mind follows, and I would not wish for Miss Bennet to be injured." Darcy studied the reins in his hands. "I know too well the devastation of a lady's spirit that can result from a man's insincere attentions."

Bingley placed a hand on Darcy's shoulder. "I could never be like him, Darcy. I would never injure any lady in such a fashion. *My* intentions are honourable." Bingley withdrew his hand and nudged his horse to begin walking. "Your concern does you credit, my friend, though I am quite put out that you would think so little of my character." He eyed Darcy with mock indignation.

Darcy grinned. "Swords at dawn?"

Bingley laughed. "I will repeat; I am not without sense. That is not a challenge that I ever intend to accept. Nor shall I accept pistols or fists. I value my life, limbs, and countenance too much, I am afraid."

*****

From *Through Every Storm*
A Pride and Prejudice Novella
by Leenie Brown

George Wickham slammed the glass down on the table. He had not meant to slam it down, but the table had somehow risen closer to his hand. He looked around the room, straining to find the barkeep. There appeared to be twice as many people here now as there had been mere minutes ago. Why could they not stay still instead of dancing in circles? He dropped his head into his hands.

"Come on, old boy, time to get you home." Colonel Nathaniel Denny hoisted his friend up to a semi-standing position and placed an arm around the drunken man to steady him. This was not the first time he had come to cart Wickham home. No, at one time, this had been a regular routine. Out of how many scrapes had Denny steered this reckless rogue?

"I dunno wanna go hum," slurred Wickham. "I wanna go to the greeve."

"It is not your time to go to the grave, Wickham. Perhaps tomorrow, but for tonight you are going home." Denny dragged him out the door into the night. A cold, early spring rain was beginning to fall. Denny helped Wickham mount his horse before pulling the hat from his friend's head. Perhaps a cold shower would help sober him up. Wickham uttered a curse and grabbed at one of the hats floating in front of him. The jerking action nearly sent him sprawling on the ground.

After manoeuvring his horse close to Wickham's, Denny helped right his friend once again. "Hold onto the saddle, old man.

I will steer you home." Wickham grabbed the saddle and slumped forward. Confident that his friend would stay seated, Denny nudged his horse to walk. With one hand on his own reigns and one on Wickham's, he began the slow journey to Wickham's rented house.

Wickham shivered as the rain ran down his face and under the collar of his coat. The coldness of the rain and the night air brought back to him the pain he had been attempting to forget. "She's gone." He lifted his head long enough to spit out the words before slumping forward once again. The effort to stay upright was still too great.

"Yes, she is gone." Denny knew what few others knew. Wickham, though once a cad and a rake, had learned to love his wife — a wife who was forced upon him due to an ill-thought out plan for revenge. Theirs had been a hard life of scraping by, first on the meager earnings of an enlisted man and then, the poor profits from his shop.

In one respect, she had been good for him. His love for her had finally overcome his love of gambling and had helped him gain a desire to become a respectable gentleman. It was too bad that she had not returned his affection.

Also by Rose Fairbanks

No Cause to Repine

Undone Business

Letters from the Heart

Sample of *The Gentleman's Impertinent Daughter*

September 30, 1811

"Come Brother, let us rest ourselves for a moment," Georgiana Darcy beseeched her elder brother. The two settled on a nearby bench.

"I am sorry Sweetling. It is very warm and I should be more attentive to you. Would you like to go home?" Fitzwilliam Darcy looked at his sister with concern. The sun was shining unseasonably hot for late September.

"No, I am well."

"I do wish you would come with me to Hertfordshire, or allow me to stay behind with you. I do not like leaving you after your ordeal just yet."

They had arrived in London only two days before, after celebrating the customary

Michaelmas feast at Pemberley, their country estate. After the betrayal of the summer and the hustle of the harvest, Darcy was looking forward to enjoying a holiday, but hated to leave his dear sister behind.

"Really, William, it was not an illness. I have simply had low spirits because of my foolishness."

Georgiana lowered her voice. "I would enjoy the countryside but I will take the cowardly way out and avoid Mr. Bingley's sisters since you offered. You know how difficult it is for me to make new friends and I do not trust my judgment in regards to their sincerity anymore. Therefore I would be trapped with the ladies all day and make you feel guilty for any enjoyment you experience. No, you go. You work so hard. Mrs. Annesley and I shall see you at Christmas."

After a short pause she added, "Now, I think I shall watch the ducks just down there."

Mr. Darcy watched his baby sister leave. She had grown into a beautiful young lady while he was unawares. Early in the summer she had been taken advantage of, her heart broken asunder, by his childhood best friend and very own father's godson.

Swept away by romance she believed herself in love and consented to an elopement.

Learning the man in question only desired her stout dowry of thirty thousand pounds and revenge on her brother made her feelings of guilt even worse than when she understood the gravity of the scandal her actions would have caused. She had not recovered her spirits and was still filled with shame and melancholy.

I was charged to protect her and I have failed her.

Nearby he heard something wholly unexpected, a full, hearty laugh from a woman. It had been years since he heard a woman laugh so openly, not since his mother's death. And the tone of this particular laugh was delightful and enchanting. Women of his circle rarely laughed unless they were belittling someone. It was a sad way to live, to be so bitter and angry.

His eyes sought out the owner of the musical laughter and saw a young woman surrounded by four children under the age of ten.

Surely she is much too young to be their mother but dressed too fine to be a governess. Though clearly she takes little care of her wardrobe, given the way she romps with the little mites. Refreshing, a young lady not interested in fashion.

He had never seen a woman with such obvious zest for life before. This lady had an inner happiness and was unafraid for the world to see it.

Acknowledgments

A special thank you goes to to my irreplaceable editor, Anna Horner. To my author friends Elizabeth, Leenie, Rosie, and Zoe that always were willing to hold my hand, nothing can take your place in my heart.

Thank you to the countless other people of the JAFF community who have inspired and encouraged me.

Last but not least I could never have written, let alone published, without the love and support of my beloved husband and babies!

About the Author

Rose Fairbanks fell in love with Mr. Fitzwilliam Darcy thirteen years ago. Coincidentally, or perhaps not, she also met her real life Mr. Darcy thirteen years ago. They had their series of missteps, just like Elizabeth and Darcy, but are now teaching the admiring multitude what happiness in marriage really looks like and have been blessed with two children, a four year old son and a two year old daughter.

Previously rereading her favorite Austen novels several times a year, Rose discovered Jane Austen Fan Fiction due to pregnancy-induced insomnia. Several months later she began writing. *Love Lasts Longest* is Rose's sixth published work.

Rose has a degree in history and hopes to one day finish her MA in Modern Europe and will focus on the Regency Era in Great Britain. For now, she gets to satiate her love of research, Pride and Prejudice, reading and writing....and the only thing she has to sacrifice is sleep! She proudly admits to her Darcy obsession, addictions to reading, chocolate and sweet tea, is always in the mood for a good debate and dearly loves to laugh.

You can connect with Rose on Facebook, Twitter, and her blog: http://rosefairbanks.com

To join her email list for information about new releases and any other news, you can sign up here: http://eepurl.com/bmJHjn

Made in the USA
Lexington, KY
04 October 2015